MR. ROGERS

Illustrated by Meryl Henderson

MR. ROGERS

by George E. Stanley

ALADDIN PAPERBACKS

New York   London   Toronto   Sydney

A special thanks to the library staff of Indiana University of Pennsylvania and to the staff of the Latrobe Presbyterian Church in Latrobe, Pennsylvania.

A heartfelt thanks to Dr. Cindy Ross, president of Cameron University, for deeds too numerous to mention. She is a true Renaissance woman.

First Aladdin Paperbacks edition September 2004
Text copyright © 2004 by George E. Stanley
Illustrations copyright © 2004 by Meryl Henderson

ALADDIN PAPERBACKS
An imprint of Simon & Schuster Children's Publishing Division
1230 Avenue of the Americas, New York, NY 10020

Designed by Lisa Vega
The text of this book was set in Adobe Garamond.

Printed and bound in the United States of America
2 4 6 8 10 9 7 5 3 1

Library of Congress Control Number 2004101192
ISBN 0-689-87186-4

ILLUSTRATIONS

CONTENTS

The Newest Citizen of Latrobe, Pennsylvania

A few minutes after 8 A.M. on Tuesday, March 20, 1928, a car stopped in front of the Latrobe Area Hospital in Latrobe, Pennsylvania. Mr. and Mrs. Fred McFeely hurriedly climbed out.

"Drive on back to the brick factory, Robert," Mr. McFeely said to the man behind the wheel. "I have no idea how long we'll be here. Our son-in-law will take us home."

"Yes, sir, Mr. McFeely," Robert said.

Mr. McFeely held the front door open for his wife, and they went inside the hospital.

"Why does Robert need our automobile?" Mrs. McFeely asked.

"I told him he could take it to Pittsburgh to check on an order," Mr. McFeely said. "One of our customers said some of the bricks we delivered last week were cracked."

"Fred, I do not understand why you continue to stay involved in the day-to-day business at the brick factory," Mrs. McFeely said. "You have a son-in-law who's quite capable of running it. In fact, James has done such a wonderful job, he and Nancy have made a fortune of their own."

"You're right, dear, and I'm quite proud of James. In fact, just the other day I heard someone in town refer to him as 'Mr. Latrobe.' I thought that was quite a compliment," Mr. McFeely said. "But after all these years, you should know that I just like to work. I'd go crazy if I weren't working."

At that moment, Mr. McFeely spotted the hospital's head nurse, Mabel Archer, whose husband was one of the foremen at the McFeely Brick Company.

"Mabel!" Mr. McFeely called. "I understand we're grandparents!"

"Mr. and Mrs. McFeely! Yes! Congratulations!" Nurse Archer said. She stopped and waited for the McFeelys to reach her. "Fred McFeely Rogers is Latrobe's newest citizen!"

Mr. McFeely turned to his wife. "Did you hear that, dear? They named him after me!"

"Well, Fred, I can't believe it's a surprise," Mrs. McFeely said. "After all, Nancy and James both said they were going to do that if it was a boy."

"Have you seen the baby yet?" Mr. McFeely asked Nurse Archer.

"Oh my, yes, and does he ever look healthy!" Nurse Archer said. "He weighed nine pounds, two ounces."

"Goodness! Is my daughter all right?" Mrs.

McFeely asked. "I knew I shouldn't have left her."

"She's just fine, Mrs. McFeely," Nurse Archer said. "You have nothing to worry about."

"You were with her all night, dear," Mr. McFeely said, "and you just went home to change clothes."

"The delivery actually went very fast," Nurse Archer said. She pulled a watch out of her pocket and looked at it. "I think Nancy's probably nursing the baby now, but she told me she wanted to see you both as soon as you got here."

"Oh, I can hardly contain my excitement," Mrs. McFeely said. "It has been so long since I've held a baby in my arms."

Mr. and Mrs. McFeely began following Nurse Archer down the corridor.

The Latrobe Area Hospital, built just eighteen years before, in 1910, was the pride not only of Latrobe but of southwestern

4

Pennsylvania. Fred McFeely was one of the civic leaders who was a driving force behind the plan to bring the best in medical care to the growing area.

Where Westmoreland County had once been mostly a coal-mining region, with the Latrobe No. 1 Mine and Coke Works the only major employer, the economic focus had begun to expand with the beginning of the twentieth century. Now, steel companies, distilleries, and brickyards were popping up all over Latrobe and the surrounding towns. Fred McFeely was happy to see this happen. Although growth certainly meant that more bricks would be needed for the new buildings, making the McFeely Brick Company one of the largest employers in Latrobe, it also created more job opportunities for the next generation, and this was just as important to Mr. McFeely.

"Here we are," Nurse Archer said. She tapped lightly on the door and pushed it open.

James had a broad grin on his face. He stood up and said, "Meet Fred McFeely Rogers! We're calling him Freddie."

"Oh, what a big, handsome boy he is!" Mrs. McFeely said.

"Of course he's handsome," Mr. McFeely said. "He's named after me."

Nancy and James laughed.

"May I hold him?" Mrs. McFeely asked.

"Well, Freddie's a handful, Mother," Nancy said, "but he doesn't seem all that interested in eating just now, so I guess it's all right." She looked up at Nurse Archer. "Is there anything unusual about that?" she asked.

Nurse Archer frowned. "Well, a newborn is usually ready to start nursing right away, but maybe Freddie wasn't hungry," she said. "I'll talk to Dr. Thomas and see what he has to say."

James took Freddie from his wife, tucked him under his chin, and looked lovingly at him for a few seconds. Just as he started to hand him to Mrs. McFeely, Freddie made a strange wheezing sound.

"What's wrong with him, James?" Nancy asked. There was deep concern in her voice. "Is he all right?"

"I don't know," James replied. He looked at Nurse Archer.

"It could have been an air bubble," Nurse Archer said. "Let me try to burp him."

Nurse Archer put the baby on her shoulder and began patting his back.

"I can't imagine what he'd have to burp," Nancy said. "He didn't nurse very long at all."

Suddenly, Freddie made a louder wheezing noise and began gasping for air.

"My baby!" Nancy cried. She struggled to sit up, but cried out in pain herself. "There's something wrong with him, James, I just know there is!"

"Let me take him to the nursery," Nurse Archer said. "He may need some oxygen."

"What does that mean?" Nancy cried.

"Nancy, darling, it's going to be all right," James told her. He took Nancy's hand and began stroking it.

"I'll go with Nurse Archer, at least as far as they'll let me," Mr. McFeely said. "Dear, you stay here with Nancy and James," he said to his wife. "I'm sure there's nothing to worry about."

Nurse Archer was already out of the room with Freddie and was hurrying down the corridor toward the nursery. "Nurse Newell! Find Dr. Thomas!" she shouted to a nurse who was coming toward her. "The Rogers baby is having trouble breathing."

"Dr. Thomas is in surgery," Nurse Newell said. "Dr. Martin is just back from doing his rounds. I'll get him."

Nurse Archer reached the door to the nursery and pushed it open with her hip. She headed immediately toward a crib with an oxygen tent.

Fred McFeely was tempted to follow her, so strong was his need to protect his new

grandson, but he didn't want to break any hospital rules. He watched from the window outside the nursery.

Just then, Dr. Martin came racing down the corridor, nodded at Mr. McFeely, and joined Nurse Archer in the nursery at the oxygen tent.

Dr. Martin put a stethoscope to Freddie's chest. He listened for a few minutes, then he went to a white metal cabinet and withdrew a syringe. Dr. Martin pinched Freddie's thigh and gave him an injection.

After several minutes, Dr. Martin turned and looked toward the nursery window where Mr. McFeely was still standing. He nodded that everything was going to be all right.

Fred McFeely hadn't realized that he was holding his breath. Slowly, he let it out.

When Dr. Martin came out of the nursery, Mr. McFeely said, "You can't let anything happen to him! You just can't!" Then he realized how that sounded and added, "I'm sorry, Dr. Martin. It's just that Freddie is our first. . . ." He couldn't continue, as his eyes began tearing and his throat tightened.

Dr. Martin patted Mr. McFeely on the shoulder. "I think we're out of the woods now, Mr. McFeely," he said. "Freddie's responding to the medicine I gave him, and Nurse Archer is going to watch him for the next few hours to make sure there's no repeat of what happened."

"We should let my daughter and her husband know," Mr. McFeely said. "Nancy's probably beside herself."

"That's where I'm going now," Dr. Martin said.

As they headed back to Room 110, the doctor said, "Mr. McFeely, your grandson is lucky to have a grandfather who's interested in making sure that the people of this part of Pennsylvania have the best medical facilities available to them."

"Thank you, Dr. Martin," Mr. McFeely said, "but this is just a cold building without such skilled physicians as yourself."

When they reached Room 110, Dr. Martin pushed open the door and found Nancy sitting up in bed, dabbing at her puffy eyes with a tissue. James and Mrs. McFeely were standing beside her.

"Where's my baby?" Nancy sobbed. "Where's my Freddie?"

"He's in the nursery, Mrs. Rogers," Dr. Martin said. "Nurse Archer is taking care of him, and I'm sure that she won't look away from him for even a second."

"Is he going to be all right, Doctor?" James asked in a shaky voice.

"I think he's going to be fine," Dr. Martin said. "I believe Freddie had an allergic reaction to something, but I gave him an injection to counteract it."

Just then, there was a knock at the door.

Mr. McFeely went over and opened it.

James's parents were standing there with a glass vase of flowers.

"Oh, Nancy, dear, we are so thrilled," Mrs. Rogers said, "but I'm sorry that we . . ." She stopped and looked around the room. "What's wrong? Where's the baby?"

"It's all right, Mother," James said. "Freddie was having a little problem breathing, and he's in the nursery now, but Dr. Martin has assured us that he'll be all right."

"I just got off work, son," Mr. Rogers said apologetically. "I'm sorry we couldn't come any sooner."

"I understand, Dad," James said. "We're just glad you're here now."

"I brought these flowers from my hothouse garden, Nancy," Mrs. Rogers said. "I hope you—"

"Well, unfortunately, I think I'm going to have to confiscate those flowers, Mrs. Rogers," Dr. Martin interrupted. He nodded to another bouquet on the chest across the room. "Those too."

Nancy looked puzzled. "Why?" she asked.

"They could be the culprit," Dr. Martin

said. "I don't know for sure yet, but the reaction that Freddie had was similar to that of people with allergies to plants."

Mrs. McFeely gasped. "Are you telling me that the roses we sent to the hospital could have killed our grandson?"

"Respiratory problems in infants are always serious, Mrs. McFeely, but I don't think it had reached that critical point," Dr. Martin said. "You're going to have to watch Freddie carefully when you take him home, though, because you never know what might trigger another reaction such as this."

"With your help, Dr. Martin, James and I will make sure that our house is free of anything that might cause this to happen again," Nancy said.

"Good," Dr. Martin said. "In the meantime, I'll take these flowers out to the waiting room."

When Dr. Martin was gone, Nancy said, "I have something to say to everyone."

"Darling, you need to rest and regain your strength," James said. "Can't it wait until tomorrow?"

"No, James, it can't," Nancy said. She took a deep breath. "I want you all to know that nothing like this will ever again happen to Freddie. I give you my solemn oath. I will always protect him and will never let him out of my sight."

Will You Be My Neighbor?

Nancy McFeely Rogers was true to her word. When she and James took Freddie home from the hospital to the great big redbrick house on Weldon Street in Latrobe, she immediately set about creating a safe world for him, especially since they had learned that Freddie did indeed have allergies.

"I just don't think I could stand it if anything happened to Freddie," she told several friends who came by to visit her. "I don't let him out of my sight for even a minute."

As the winter of 1929 and 1930 turned into

the spring of 1930, things were not going well for the economy of the United States. What came to be called the Great Depression had begun. In Latrobe, some of the stores suffered, but most people went on with their lives as best they could. There was concern but not gloom in the Rogers' household. Financially, they were in very good shape.

At times, Freddie's room resembled a toy store. If his parents saw something in a magazine that they thought he would enjoy playing with or that would help improve his dexterity or teach him an important skill, they bought it. If the stores in Latrobe or Pittsburgh didn't have a particular item, Freddie's mother ordered it from the Sears catalog. Boxes of wooden blocks, trucks, and other toys arrived regularly at the Rogers' house.

Freddie spent most of 1931 in and out of the hospital because of his respiratory problems, but now Dr. Thomas was also concerned that

Freddie was gaining too much weight.

"I know he needs to get more exercise outside," Mrs. Rogers told Dr. Thomas one afternoon when he came by the house to examine Freddie, "but I make him stay inside because all the dust and pollen is bad for his hay fever."

"I do understand your dilemma, Mrs. Rogers," Dr. Thomas said, "so you might think about cutting back on the portions of food that you serve Freddie at each meal."

One summer evening in 1932, when his McFeely grandparents had come for dinner, Freddie was sure that his father and his grandfather would want to see the town he had built with his wooden blocks. His mother had shown him a picture of some of the tall buildings in Pittsburgh, and Freddie had stacked his blocks as high as they would go without falling. His favorite game now was "Let's go to Pittsburgh."

After dinner, when Freddie had washed up and changed from the dress clothes he wore when his family had guests into his play clothes, he went downstairs and found his father and grandfather sitting in the parlor by the radio.

Freddie started to ask them if they wanted to play with him, but he stopped before any words came out of his mouth.

Freddie knew he had to use his manners. One of the most important rules in his family was that young people did not interrupt adults. Freddie was expected to sit and listen and not speak until he was spoken to.

Freddie sat down in a velvet chair next to a small table on which his mother had some of her favorite figurines. After a while, when Freddie had decided that the man on the radio wasn't going to stop talking anytime soon, he looked over at the figurines and wondered what they would be thinking if they were alive.

The man was a shepherd, his mother had told him once, and the woman was a shepherdess. Together, they took care of the flock of sheep that surrounded them on the table.

Freddie reached out and moved one of the sheep so that it was on the other side of the lamp. He turned the shepherd so that he was facing the shepherdess. "One of the lambs is missing," Freddie whispered, pretending to be the voice of the shepherd. "We have to find it or the wolves will eat it."

The base of the lamp was sculpted, so that if you really pretended hard, it looked like rocks piled at the bottom of a mountain.

"Yes, one of us must go right now," Freddie the shepherdess whispered. "There are many wolves here, and they are always looking for little lambs."

"I'll go," Freddie the shepherd said. "You stay with the rest of the sheep."

"Oh, I should really go myself," Freddie

the shepherdess said. "I was supposed to take care of that lamb, but I turned my head to look up at the stars. I should be the one to go find it."

Just then, Freddie's father stood up and turned off the radio. "I know the news keeps sounding worse and worse, Mr. McFeely," he said, "but we've weathered the storm so far, and I still think we'll be fine at the brick factory."

"President Hoover should have seen this Depression coming, but he obviously didn't," Mr. McFeely said. "The only ones who can save this country now are the Democrats."

Mr. Rogers shook his head sadly. "What will become of all those poor families now that the fathers are gone?"

"I don't understand how things could be so bad that a man would jump out of a window," Grandfather McFeely said. "That's no solution to the problem. Now their families will only suffer more."

Freddie suddenly felt something funny in

his chest. That happened once in a while, but it was usually after a meal or when he had been outside to play. Quickly, he moved the figurines back to their original places on the table. He would have to finish this story later.

Freddie left the parlor and went in search of his mother. He had an important question to ask her.

Mrs. Rogers and Grandmother McFeely were still in the kitchen. They were sitting at the table, drinking coffee, and leafing through a book of recipes.

Freddie's mother looked up when he came into the room. "Why, Freddie, you're as pale as a ghost," she said. "Darling, what's wrong? Don't you feel well?"

Freddie climbed up into his mother's lap. "Papa won't ever jump out of a window and leave us, will he, Mama?" he asked, his voice choking.

Grandmother McFeely gasped.

"Oh my goodness, no!" Mrs. Rogers said. "Whatever gave you that idea?"

Freddie told her what he had heard when he was in the parlor.

"Darling, that would never happen to our family," Mrs. Rogers said.

As his mother rocked him back and forth, Freddie felt himself relaxing. He remembered the shepherd and the shepherdess and the lost lamb. The story had an ending after all, he realized. He was the lamb, and his mother was the shepherdess. She had found him, and he was safe and secure.

"Sometimes I think I'll take all of the radios out of our house," Grandmother McFeely said. "There's nothing but bad news on them these days."

"I know, Mother. I really just want to listen to the programs that make me laugh," Mrs. Rogers said, "but then we wouldn't know about all of the suffering in the world, and I think it's important that we remember those who aren't as fortunate as we are."

Grandmother McFeely sighed. "As usual, you're right, Nancy," she said. "We must always keep that in mind."

Freddie's mother looked down at him. "Just remember this, sweetheart. When you hear things that frighten you, look for helpers," she said. "You'll always find people who are willing to help you."

At first, Freddie wasn't quite sure what his mother meant, but the more he thought about it, the more it seemed to make sense. His parents were always around to make sure he felt safe. So were both sets of grandparents.

But Freddie suddenly realized that helpers didn't have to be real people. The shepherd and the shepherdess weren't real, but in his mind, Freddie had made them real. He could talk to them not only about the problems they had herding their flock of sheep but about what they did when they heard things on the radio that frightened them.

After all, Freddie told himself, since the two figurines were on the table in the parlor where the big radio was, they heard everything that was said.

One day in October 1933, when Freddie's Grandmother McFeely came to his house to have tea with his mother, she said, "Look at that child, Nancy! He's created an entire city out of those wooden blocks."

"Oh, yes, Mother! I thought I had told you about it. This is Pittsburgh, and Freddie's favorite game is still 'Let's go to Pittsburgh,'" Mrs. Rogers said. "I was just about to play it with him. Would you care to join us?"

"I'd be delighted to," Grandmother McFeely said.

Mrs. Rogers and Grandmother McFeely sat down on the floor beside Freddie.

"You drive the truck, Nana," Freddie said. "Mama, you drive this car."

"Oh, my goodness," Grandmother McFeely

said. "I've never driven a truck before. I'm not sure I know how."

"You just *pretend* to drive it, Nana," Freddie said. "If you pretend, you can do anything you want to do."

"Well, I suppose that's true, dear," Grandmother McFeely said.

For the next hour, the three of them drove back and forth between Latrobe and Pittsburgh. Freddie told them what kind of business was in each building.

His mother and grandmother parked in front of one and went inside to buy some new clothes. At another one, they bought ice-cream cones.

Freddie pointed to the biggest building. "This is a toy store," he said. "I go here all the time."

Mrs. Rogers and Grandmother McFeely laughed.

Finally, Grandmother McFeely said, "Oh, I have to stand up, Freddie, if I can. I'm getting stiff just sitting down here on the floor like this."

Mrs. Rogers stood up first and then helped her mother up.

"Can't you play with me some more, Nana?" Freddie asked.

"No, dear, we've just hired a new cook and I need to go home and make sure that dinner has been started," Grandmother McFeely said. "I've taken up too much of your mother's time already."

"But I was going to build a brick factory just like the one Papa and Ding Dong work in," Freddie said.

"Ding Dong?" Grandmother McFeely said. She turned to Mrs. Rogers. "Where in the world did Freddie come up with that nickname for your father?"

"It's from that nursery rhyme that Father reads to him all the time," Mrs. Rogers said. "You know the one. He read it to me when I was Freddie's age. 'Ding Dong Dell, Pussy's in the well . . .' Freddie just loves it."

"Ah, yes," Grandmother McFeely said. She turned back to Freddie. "Why don't you build *Ding Dong* something else, dear? If there's one thing your grandfather doesn't need, it's another brick factory. He already has five of them."

Mrs. Rogers laughed. "How do you stand it, Mother? Father's been talking about buying chickens and cattle and even another coal mine. I've never ever heard him mention the word 'retirement.'"

"Nancy, your father would die if he weren't working," Grandmother McFeely said. "He's told me that a million times, so I don't even bring it up anymore."

After his mother and grandmother left the room, Freddie thought about what his grandmother had said, that his grandfather would die if he didn't work, and Freddie knew he had to talk to somebody about that. *But whom?* he wondered.

Suddenly, Freddie remembered the bottom drawer of a chest in one of the guest bedrooms. His mother kept old socks and other articles of clothing there to use as dust rags.

Freddie climbed the stairs to the bedroom, opened the bottom drawer of the chest, and pulled out a white work sock. He held it up and looked at it. *This will work,* he thought.

He put his hand inside the sock and moved it around. "Hello, Freddie!" he said in a disguised voice. "I'm your new friend!"

That made Freddie laugh. But the sock needed a face, so Freddie took it downstairs to his father's study and got a bottle of ink. With one of his father's fountain pens, he drew two circles on the sock to make the eyes. He made a half circle for the nose, and a straight line for the mouth.

"What's your name?" Freddie asked the sock.

"Well, what do you want my name to be?" the sock asked.

Freddie thought for a minute. All of a sudden, he had a wonderful idea. "How about *Mr. McFeely*?" he said.

"Oh, that's your grandfather's name, isn't it?" the sock said. "Why do you want me to have the same name he has?"

"If you're Mr. McFeely, then I can ask you all of the things that I would ask Ding Dong if he were here," Freddie said.

"Why can't my name be 'Ding Dong'?" the sock asked.

"There can be only one Ding Dong," Freddie said. "I want you to be Mr. McFeely."

"All right. My name is Mr. McFeely," the sock said. "Ask me my first question."

"Why does my grandfather have to die?" Freddie asked.

"Why do you think he's going to die?" Mr. McFeely said.

"Grandmother said that if he didn't work, he'd die," Freddie said. "I don't want him to die."

Freddie made the sock look around the room. "Do you see your grandfather anywhere in here?"

"No," Freddie said.

"Where is he?" Mr. McFeely asked.

"He's at the brick factory with Papa," Freddie replied.

"Tell me what your grandfather looks like," Mr. McFeely said.

Freddie described his grandfather to the sock.

"Now, tell me where else your grandfather is," Mr. McFeely said.

"I don't understand you," Freddie said. "He's at the brick factory with Papa. He isn't anywhere else."

"Then how did you know what your grandfather looks like?" Mr. McFeely asked. "He's not in this room, so you can't *see* him."

Suddenly Freddie brightened. "He's inside my head!" he shouted.

Freddie moved the sock's head up and

down. "That's right," Mr. McFeely said. He looked Freddie straight in the eye. "Everyone has to die one of these days, Freddie, but your grandfather will always be inside your head."

Freddie lowered his hand. He knew that the sock wasn't real, so where had Mr. McFeely's words come from? *If you pretend to be somebody else, do different thoughts come into your head?* Freddie wondered. What an amazing thing that was! he decided.

Over the next few weeks, Freddie was sick and had to stay in bed a lot, but with his Mr. McFeely puppet to keep him company and talk to him about things that were on his mind, he wasn't bored at all.

Finally, he began to feel better, and his mother let him sit on the back porch. One day, Freddie smelled something wonderful coming from the kitchen window of Mama Bell Framton's house next door. It made him hungry. Freddie had to find out what it was.

Freddie left the porch, walked to a side gate that would let him into Mama Bell Framton's backyard, and knocked on her door.

"Well, hello, Freddie, how are you feeling, dear?" Mama Bell Framton said. "Your mother said you'd been under the weather."

"I'm feeling really well now, Mama Bell," Freddie said, "but I think I'd feel even better if I had some of whatever it is you're cooking."

Mama Bell gave a hearty laugh. "Toast sticks! That's what I'm cooking, Freddie," she said. "So come on in and help me eat them, because I certainly want to make sure you're feeling even better!"

Mama Bell showed Freddie how to put the bread in the toaster. After that, she showed him how to spread the butter and jam on the toast. Then, with her help, Freddie cut the toast into four long "sticks."

Mama Bell poured Freddie a glass of milk and herself another cup of tea, and together they sat at the table and ate their toast sticks.

When they finished, Freddie said, "Thank you for the toast sticks, Mama Bell. Papa and Mama are always talking about what a wonderful neighbor you are to them. Will you be my neighbor too?"

"I would be honored to be your neighbor, Freddie," Mama Bell said.

King Sneezer

Since music had always been important in the lives of the McFeelys and the Rogerses, no one in the family thought there was anything unusual about Freddie's wanting to sit on the stool in front of the piano in the parlor when he was five and "pretend to play."

At first, Freddie's "songs" were just random notes, but after a while, they started to sound like familiar tunes. Freddie began to attract an audience of family admirers.

"Of course I recognize that song," Grandmother McFeely said to him one afternoon in 1934. "It's 'Blue Moon.'"

Freddie grinned at his grandmother. "You're right, Nana!" he said. "I heard it on the radio last night." He turned around and started playing another song. "Tell me if you know what this one is."

After listening to several bars, Grandmother McFeely said, "'Anything Goes'!"

"You're right again, Nana!" Freddie said.

Grandmother McFeely turned to Mrs. Rogers and said, "Nancy, you may have a child prodigy here. This is not a game with Freddie, my dear. He's beginning to understand music."

"I know, Mother, and I think it's wonderful," Mrs. Rogers said. "I've already talked to Miss Johnson at church, and she's agreed to start working with Freddie one day a week."

Grandmother McFeely and Mrs. Rogers listened to several more songs to see if they could guess what they were, then Mrs.

Rogers said, "Mother, I want to show you my Christmas project. I'll be right back."

"All right, dear," Grandmother McFeely said.

After his mother had left the room, Freddie said, "Nana, listen to this."

Freddie began striking notes all up and down the piano, but he lingered on the low notes. Unlike the songs he had just played for his mother and grandmother, these notes were loud and sounded like thunder. When he finished his song, Freddie turned to his grandmother and said, "Well, Nana? Did you like it?"

"It's a very pretty song, Freddie," Grandmother McFeely said, "but I don't recognize the tune."

Freddie grinned. "That's because I made it up," he said. "I make up a lot of songs."

"That's wonderful, dear," Grandmother McFeely said. "What is the name of it?"

"'I'm Angry!'" Freddie replied.

"Oh, well, are you angry?" Grandmother McFeely asked.

Freddie shook his head. "Not now, Nana," he replied. "If I play that song, I'm not angry anymore."

Freddie turned around and started playing another song. This time, he mostly played high notes, and he didn't strike the keys as hard or as long.

When Freddie finished, he said, "How do I feel when I play that song, Nana?"

"It doesn't sound sad like the other song. In fact, I thought I could hear people laughing," Grandmother McFeely said. "I think you're happy when you play that song."

Freddie nodded. "You're right," he said. "I can do all of this with my fingers. I can be happy, and I can be sad. I can laugh, and I can cry."

Just then, Mrs. Rogers returned with a knitting bag in her hands.

"Freddie has been playing some of his original compositions for me, Nancy," Grandmother McFeely said. "He makes up songs to fit how he feels. They're actually quite good. In fact, I've been thinking that it might be a very good way for all of us to deal with our emotions."

"What's that, Mama?" Freddie asked. He hopped down from the piano stool and joined his mother and grandmother on the sofa.

"It's a Christmas gift," Mrs. Rogers said, "but since it isn't your gift, I can show it to you."

Mrs. Rogers pulled a bundle of green yarn out of the knitting bag and held it up.

"Oh, my goodness, Nancy!" Grandmother McFeely exclaimed. "What an absolutely gorgeous sweater!"

"What do you think about the fish on the front?" Mrs. Rogers asked.

Grandmother McFeely pulled the sweater closer to her and examined the white band with the row of gray fish. "They're extremely well done, dear," she said. "I'm quite impressed." She looked up. "I knew you could knit, Nancy, but I never knew you could knit this *well*. The sweaters that you see in the better department stores in Pittsburgh aren't nearly of this quality."

"Oh, Mother, you're exaggerating," Mrs. Rogers said. She hesitated. "Aren't you?" she asked expectantly.

"No, dear, I'm not," Grandmother McFeely said.

Mrs. Rogers turned to Freddie. "What do you think of it, Freddie?" she asked.

"I wish I had one like it," Freddie said.

Mrs. Rogers smiled at him. "Well, sometimes wishes do come true, dear," she said. "But this sweater is for Grandfather Rogers. Do you think he'll like it?"

"Oh, yes! He likes green, and he likes to fish!" Freddie said. "This will be a wonderful Christmas present for him."

"You should be quite proud of yourself, Nancy," Grandmother McFeely said. "That is an excellent Christmas project."

"Oh, this is just part of the project, Mother," Mrs. Rogers said. "What I actually plan to do is knit one sweater each month until Christmas to give as gifts to family and friends."

"They'll be cherished, I know, and quite warm to wear," Mrs. McFeely said. "I guess I need to start thinking of what I should be doing too." She sighed. "We're quite fortunate, not having the financial troubles that this horrible Depression has caused most people, but we still need to be good stewards of what we've been blessed with."

"Those were my feelings too, Mother," Mrs. Rogers said. "There may come a day when we'll need to help some of our less fortunate family members and friends through the more difficult times that I'm sure are still to come."

While his mother and grandmother continued to talk about other matters, Freddie thought about the Christmas he had just enjoyed with his Grandmother and Grandfather Rogers. It was always a special event.

It was only January now, Freddie knew, and that meant that the next Christmas was a long way away, but he could hardly wait to taste his Grandmother Rogers's wonderful stuffing.

Freddie closed his eyes and, all of a sudden, in his head, it was Christmas Eve again, and he and his parents had just arrived for dinner.

"I made several bowls of stuffing just for you, Freddie," Grandmother Rogers whispered to him.

"Oh, thank you!" Freddie told her. He looked around to see if anybody else was listening, then he whispered, "What about corn pudding? Did you make some of that?"

"Of course, I did!" Grandmother Rogers said. "It wouldn't be Christmas for you if I didn't make corn pudding, now would it?"

"No, Grandma," Freddie said. "I wouldn't even care if that's all we had, stuffing and corn pudding."

"Well, I think you and I could get away with that, dear," Grandmother Rogers said, "but I'm not quite sure we'd make everyone else very happy if we left out the rest of the dinner."

Freddie grinned. "I guess I would be unhappy too," he told her.

Just then, his grandfather Rogers gave him a big hug and asked, "When are you and I going fishing, Freddie?"

"Isn't the water too cold to go fishing now, Grandpa?" Freddie asked.

"We could go *ice* fishing," Grandpa Rogers said. "If we did that, you wouldn't be around all that stuff that makes you sneeze." He turned to Freddie's mother. "What about it, Nancy? Why don't you let me take this boy ice fishing?"

"Oh, Grandpa Rogers, Freddie can't go ice fishing," Mrs. Rogers said. "He'd get pneumonia. I'm sure his lungs will get stronger one of these days. That's what I've read, and that's what the doctors all say, but until then, I just don't like exposing him to things that might make him sick."

Freddie could tell that his grandfather Rogers was disappointed, and he was actually disappointed too. But Freddie didn't like it when he couldn't breathe very well and had to sit in a room with pots of water boiling on the stove, or when his mother rubbed some of that awful-smelling salve on his chest.

"I promise I'll go fishing with you one of these days, Grandpa Rogers," Freddie said. "I promise."

"Freddie! Freddie! What's wrong?"

Freddie opened his eyes. He was back in the parlor of his house, and his mother and grandmother McFeely were looking at him with concern.

"Oh, nothing, Mama," Freddie said. "I was just thinking about how wonderful Christmas always is."

❖ ❖ ❖ ❖

Over the next few months, as the leaves on the trees began budding and the flowers and the grass began poking up through the earth, Freddie had to stay inside to keep his hay fever under control. He spent a lot of time playing the toy piano Grandmother McFeely had bought him. He also read from the many books his parents gave him, and he enjoyed listening to some of the musical programs on the radio. But most of all, he liked making puppets.

Ever since Freddie made his first puppet, his family had begun giving him old socks and paper bags. He now had ten puppets made from socks and three from paper bags. He had also discovered that pieces of colored cloth made better faces than ink. Because Freddie was color-blind, which meant he couldn't tell one color from another, his mother helped him choose colors for the eyes and noses and mouths. Then she either sewed them onto the socks or glued them onto the paper bags where Freddie told her to. On this particular day, they were sitting together in her sewing room getting ready to make the newest addition to Freddie's puppet collection.

"Who is coming to live with us today?" Mrs. Rogers asked.

"This is King Sneezer," Freddie said. "He sneezes for other people so they won't have to."

Mrs. Rogers smiled. "Welcome, King Sneezer," she said.

"He needs a crown, Mama," Freddie said, "and I think he needs a red nose, too, because he sneezes all the time."

Mrs. Rogers opened a drawer in a chest next to her sewing machine and began pulling out pieces of colored cloth. "I think I have just what King Sneezer needs," she said.

When Mrs. Rogers had finished with the puppet, Freddie stuck his hand inside the sock, and King Sneezer said, "Thank you very

much for my crown and my face. I am very happy to be here."

"You're welcome, King Sneezer," Mrs. Rogers said. "I'm glad that you—"

Just then, the telephone rang downstairs.

Mrs. Rogers looked at the clock on the wall. "I wonder who that could be," she said.

When the telephone continued to ring, Mrs. Rogers said, "Oh, dear, I told Ruth when we hired her to keep house that one of her duties would be to answer the telephone when I was upstairs. She must still be outside, hanging out the wash. Will you please answer it for me, Freddie? And remember to use your best manners, all right?"

"Yes, Mama," Freddie said.

He took King Sneezer off his hand and went downstairs.

When he reached the telephone, he stood on the stool his parents had put there just for him and took the receiver off the hook. "This is the home of Mr. and Mrs. James Rogers and their son, Fred McFeely Rogers," Freddie said. "This is Fred McFeely Rogers speaking."

"Freddie, it's Grandma Rogers," the voice said, but Freddie had never heard his grandmother sound like this before. "I need to speak to your mother. It's very important, dear. Could you please get her for me?"

"Yes, Grandma," Freddie said. He laid the receiver on the table by the telephone. He knew he wasn't supposed to run in the house or up the stairs, but something inside him told him that this time it would be all right.

Freddie hurried up the stairs as fast as he could. "Mama! Mama!" he called. "It's Grandma Rogers. She sounds funny."

Mrs. Rogers met him at the door of the sewing room. "All right, Freddie, thank you," she said.

Freddie followed his mother back downstairs. He watched as his mother picked up the receiver. "Mother Rogers? Is everything all right?" his mother said. She listened for just a minute, then she let out a sob. "Oh, Mother Rogers, I am so sorry. Does James know yet?"

Outside, Freddie heard his father's car coming into the driveway. Instantly, he knew that something really terrible had happened. His father never came home this early. Freddie was sure that the reason had to do with the telephone call from his grandmother Rogers.

The front door opened, and Mr. Rogers came inside. Freddie couldn't remember ever seeing his father's face look like it did now.

"What's wrong, Papa?" Freddie asked.

Mr. Rogers walked over and picked up Freddie and held him tight. Mrs. Rogers joined them. For several minutes, no one said anything, and Freddie could feel his heart pounding from fear. He didn't know what to do. He was scared, and he had never before been scared inside his own house. This was where he felt safe. This was where he felt protected.

"Grandpa Rogers died today," Mr. Rogers said. "It was all very sudden. Nobody expected it."

Mr. Rogers set Freddie down beside Mrs. Rogers. Without saying anything else, he started up the stairs.

Mrs. Rogers put her hand around Freddie's shoulder.

"How could Grandpa die, Mama?" Freddie asked. "I haven't gone fishing with him yet."

Mrs. Rogers let out a muffled sob. After a few minutes, she said, "Remember what I told you once, Freddie. When you're upset about something, find helpers. There is always someone willing to help you."

Freddie knew who his helpers were. They were upstairs in his room. He would talk to all of his puppets and see what they had to say about Grandpa Rogers.

The following day, Grandpa Rogers's casket was brought to his house so that family and friends could come by and pay their respects. Freddie listened as everyone told his grandmother Rogers nice things about his grandfather. He wanted to say something to her too, but he couldn't think of anything. He wished that he had brought one of his puppets with him. He was sure that it would know the right words to use.

That evening, when the clock in the parlor struck nine, Mrs. Rogers said, "We should go home now, Freddie. We have to be up early for the funeral tomorrow. Will you go find your father for me?"

"Yes, Mama," Freddie said.

Freddie looked in every room on the first floor, but his father wasn't in any of them, so he went upstairs.

As he turned a corner, he saw his father standing outside his grandparents' bedroom. Tears were streaming down his face. Freddie had never seen his father cry before. But now he knew why his father often told him that it was all right to cry: He wasn't just saying something to make Freddie feel better—it was something he actually believed.

Puppet School

"Freddie. It's time to get up," Mrs. Rogers said. "Today's a very special day."

Freddie opened his eyes and saw his mother smiling at him. "I was dreaming about Grandpa and Grandma Rogers," he said. He coughed a couple of times. "I really miss them a lot, Mama."

"We all do, dear," Mrs. Rogers said. "No one expected your grandmother to die just a few months after your grandfather." She felt Freddie's forehead. "You're a little warm," she said. "I hope you're not getting a fever."

"I feel all right, Mama," Freddie said. Quickly, he got out of bed. "May I take King Sneezer to school with me?"

"I don't think Miss Albert would mind if you did that, dear," Mrs. Rogers said. She gave Freddie a quick hug. "Miss Albert was our teacher, too, your father and I, and she's a very nice lady. She told me she was really looking forward to having you in her class."

When Freddie finished dressing, he went downstairs, had breakfast with his parents, and then they drove him to Second Ward Elementary School.

"Don't you have to go to work today, Papa?" Freddie asked.

"Yes, son, I do, but not before your mother and I make sure you've started your first day at school," Mr. Rogers replied. "This is a very important event in your life and ours."

Just as Mr. Rogers pulled in front of the school and parked, Freddie sneezed again. "That was King Sneezer," he said. "When he sneezes for me, I don't get sick."

"Well, you keep letting him sneeze for you, then," Mrs. Rogers said. "Just make sure he covers his mouth and nose so other people won't get his germs."

"Mama! I don't have to tell him that," Freddie said. "Kings have very good manners."

Freddie's parents smiled.

"You're right, Freddie," Mr. Rogers said. "We should have known that."

Inside the school, Miss Albert greeted the Rogerses and gave Freddie a big hug. "My, how time passes," she said. "Freddie, I still remember the first day of school for your parents. I've been looking forward to nineteen thirty-five and this day ever since you were born. Would you like to meet the other children?"

"Yes, ma'am," Freddie said.

Freddie kissed his mother and father good-bye, took Miss Albert's hand, and let her lead him into the classroom.

Freddie couldn't remember ever seeing so many children in one place. He didn't have any first cousins, and had just a few second and third cousins he would occasionally see in the summer, when distant relatives came to visit his grandparents. Since he wasn't allowed to play outside by himself, he didn't really know all that many children who lived in the neighborhood.

Miss Albert took Freddie to his desk and introduced him to the rest of the class. Freddie thought everyone looked really nice, and he was excited about talking to them. He especially liked Martha, who sat in the desk beside him, because Martha sneezed right after she said her name.

Suddenly, a bell rang. "That's the school bell, children," Miss Albert said. "When you hear that, you must all be quiet and listen to what I'm saying to you."

For the rest of the day, Freddie's class put

away their supplies, drew pictures, and listened to stories Miss Albert read to them. During recess, Freddie and Martha stayed inside because Miss Albert said, "There's still a lot of pollen in the air, and it will really make your hay fever worse."

When Freddie showed King Sneezer to Martha, she said, "Does he really sneeze for you?"

"Yes," Freddie said. "But he does a lot more than that, Martha."

"*He does?*" Martha said.

Freddie nodded. "Puppets are helpers. My mother said so. You can talk to puppets, and puppets can talk to you, and they can help you solve your problems."

"I get really mad because I'm sick a lot," Martha said. "Would a puppet make me feel better?"

"My puppets make me feel better all the time," Freddie said.

Suddenly, he had an idea. He opened his

satchel and took out one of the old socks he had brought with him. "We're going to make a puppet for you."

"Really? How do you do it?" Martha asked.

"We'll need scissors, glue, and construction paper," Freddie said. "I'll let you tell me which colors you want to use for the eyes, the mouth, and the nose."

"I don't care," Martha said. "You choose them."

"I can't. I'm color-blind," Freddie said. "You'd better pick out the ones you want, or your puppet might look really funny."

Martha laughed. "I want blue eyes and a red mouth and a pink nose," she said. "My puppet is going to be *Queen* Sneezer."

"Oh, that's a wonderful idea!" Freddie said.

Martha handed Freddie sheets of blue, red, and pink construction paper and told him which was which.

Freddie cut out two blue eyes, a pink nose,

and a red mouth. He let Martha glue them onto the sock.

"Queen Sneezer needs a crown too," Freddie said.

"I can make that," Martha said. She cut a crown out of a piece of gray construction paper and glued it onto Queen Sneezer's head.

They had just finished when recess was over.

Several kids wanted to see what their puppets did, so Miss Albert asked Freddie and Martha if they'd come to the front of the room and show everyone.

"I don't want to," Martha whispered to Freddie. "I don't like to talk in front of people."

"You won't be talking, Martha," Freddie whispered back. "Queen Sneezer will."

Martha thought about that for a minute. "Oh, okay," she said.

Freddie and Martha put their puppets on

their hands and walked to the front of the room.

As King Sneezer, Freddie said, "I go around the world breathing all the pollen that the trees and flowers and grass make, so that boys and girls won't have to do it, but there is so much. Queen Sneezer, will you be able to help me?"

For just a minute, Martha said nothing, then all of a sudden she got a big grin on her face. She moved her hand and fingers around so it looked as though Queen Sneezer were thinking, then she said, "Yes, King Sneezer, I'll be happy to help you. I'm not just the queen. I'm also your friend."

Freddie loved school, but he occasionally had to stay home because he was too sick to go. Miss Albert would always come by his house after school and tell his mother what work they had done that day, so he wouldn't fall behind.

On the days that Freddie couldn't go to

school, he would imagine he was there while he was sitting in his bed. He thought it would be more fun if his puppets could all be there with him. He didn't know how they could, though, since he only had two hands. One day, he saw Ruth coming up from the cellar with several jars of fruits and vegetables that she and his mother had canned during the previous summer. That gave Freddie an idea.

"Ruth, are there any empty jars I may have?" Freddie asked.

"Now don't tell me you're planning to start canning, Freddie," Ruth said.

"No, I want them for my puppets," Freddie said.

"Well, yes, there are a lot of empty jars in the cellar," Ruth said. "How many do you want?"

Freddie thought about it for a minute. "Ten," he replied.

Later that day, Ruth brought up ten empty

jars and put them in Freddie's room. Freddie took King Sneezer and pulled the sock over the jar.

"It works!" Freddie cried. "King Sneezer can sit up by himself!"

From that day on, when Freddie couldn't go to school, he would put the ten puppet jars at the foot of his bed, lined up, as though they were sitting in desks, and have school. The puppets would spell all of the words that Freddie was learning to spell. They would sing all of the songs that Freddie was learning to sing. They would write all of the letters that Freddie was learning to write. If they did well and behaved, Freddie would tell them a story.

If Freddie didn't feel well enough to be the teacher, he would put King Sneezer beside him and let King Sneezer be the teacher. In his head, Freddie thought King Sneezer made a very good teacher.

❈ ❈ ❈ ❈

puddle
round

Music continued to be very important to Freddie. Now he was playing not only the piano, but also a toy organ Grandmother McFeely bought for him as a gift because she had been so impressed that Freddie had been willing to save part of his weekly allowance to help buy it.

"I know how much you love listening to the organ at church and that you've wanted to have an organ of your own, Freddie," Grandmother McFeely said. "Now you can play hymns just like our church organist does."

Each Sunday, Freddie would pay very close attention to the hymns that the organist at the Latrobe Presbyterian Church played for the services. As soon as he got home, he would go up to his room and try to play the hymns on his organ. It wasn't long before his parents said that he sounded just like the church organist.

❉   ❉   ❉   ❉

The closer it got to spring that year, the worse Freddie's hay fever became. Sometimes he missed several weeks of school at a time. He didn't fall behind since Miss Albert brought by his homework and even tutored him occasionally. Still, Mr. and Mrs. Rogers decided that something drastic had to be done.

"I had a talk with Dr. Martin today," Mr. Rogers said one evening at dinner. "I think we may have a solution to Freddie's hay fever problem."

"What does he think will work?" Mrs. Rogers asked.

Mr. Rogers took a clipping out of the breast pocket of his jacket and handed it to Mrs. Rogers. "Dr. Martin found this advertisement in a recent issue of *Time*," he said.

"The Weather Maker," Mrs. Rogers read. "An air conditioner for private home use." She looked up. "Well, I know we've talked about getting an air conditioner, but I thought they were still mostly for cooling larger places, like department stores and factories."

"No, these smaller units have actually been around since nineteen twenty-eight, but the Depression slowed sales so much that it was difficult to get one. Here in Pennsylvania, it's just not that hot for very long, so I never thought it would be worth the investment. With an air conditioner, though, you don't need to leave the windows open in the summer, which means you don't get a lot of pollen and dust inside."

"Oh, James, it would be so wonderful if Freddie could spend an entire summer without suffering from hay fever," Mrs. Rogers said.

"Does that sound like a good idea to you, Freddie?" Mr. Rogers said.

Freddie nodded. "I'd really like it," he said. "I think King Sneezer would like it too," he added. "I know he gets tired of sneezing for me."

Unfortunately, when Mr. and Mrs. Rogers tried to order an air conditioner for Freddie's room, they were told that the company couldn't keep up with the demand and that it would be several months before it could be shipped. But Dr. Martin told them that another family in Latrobe—the Emersons, whose son suffered from asthma—had been lucky enough to get one of the Weather Makers. It was supposed to arrive in just a few days. It would be the first home air conditioner in town.

The Emersons weren't as wealthy as the Rogerses, and buying an air conditioner meant quite a financial sacrifice for them. Dr. Martin suggested that he and the two families share the cost.

The Emersons were glad to have some help paying for the air conditioner. But they didn't understand how that was going to help Freddie.

"We thought that perhaps Freddie and your son Paul could share Paul's room this summer," Mr. Rogers said.

"If Freddie and Paul can spend an entire

summer without having hay fever or asthma," Dr. Martin said, "then maybe their bodies will have time to heal themselves instead of working overtime fighting to rid them of all the things that trigger these conditions. It just might cure them."

"Oh, Dr. Martin, if that is a possible result of this, then we'll cooperate in any way necessary," Mrs. Emerson said.

As soon as school was out, Freddie moved into Paul's room for the summer. It was the biggest bedroom in the Emersons' house. His parents had furnished it so that it could easily accommodate friends who spent the night there.

"It's difficult for Paul to stay at his friends' houses, because he could have an attack of asthma at any time, and it's very important that it be dealt with immediately," Mrs. Emerson explained. "So my husband and I wanted to make sure that he had plenty of room for guests."

Since Paul's room had two of almost everything—twin beds, twin dressers, and two closets—Freddie had to move only his personal things. He also brought with him his toy organ and all of his puppets.

Mr. and Mrs. Rogers visited him every day, bringing him books to read and new materials to make even more puppets.

When Freddie asked Paul if he wanted to help him make his puppets, Paul politely told him he was too old for such things.

"I don't think anybody is too old for puppets," Freddie said. "I know a lot of adults on radio who have puppets."

But that didn't impress Paul. He went back to the book he was reading.

It didn't take Freddie long to realize that Paul wasn't happy about having him spend the summer in his room. He knew Paul was several years older than he was, but he often played with people older than him, like his parents or Nana and Ding Dong. They were always ready to talk to him and play games with him. Freddie was really disappointed.

Finally, the summer was over, and Dr. Martin announced that the experiment was a success. Freddie didn't have hay fever, and Paul didn't have an attack of asthma.

A week before school was to start in September, Freddie packed all of his belongings so he could move back to his house. He had made it through the summer, even though Paul had ignored him most of the time. Freddie had thought of his summer at the Emersons as an adventure, and he had had plenty of company with his puppets and his toy organ.

When Freddie got home, his McFeely grandparents were in the parlor. They were standing beside a real organ.

"Oh, Nana! Ding Dong!" Freddie exclaimed. "Where did this come from?"

"My dear boy, it's a reward for staying

in the air-conditioned room all summer," Grandmother McFeely said. "We are so proud of you."

"We have another surprise in your room, Freddie," Mrs. Rogers said. "Let's go on upstairs, and then you can play us a hymn on your new organ."

Freddie followed his parents and grandparents upstairs. He couldn't imagine what the other surprise was. As they neared his room, though, the familiar hum gave away the secret, but he didn't say anything.

Mr. Rogers opened the door, and everyone was greeted by a rush of pleasantly cool air.

"Now you have your own air conditioner," Mr. Rogers said.

Freddie hugged both of his parents. "Oh, thank you," he said.

"You won't have to spend a summer at Paul's house again," Mrs. Rogers said. "You can stay in your own home, and your father and I are happy about that, because we missed you very much."

Freddie was happy too. This house was his world, and he enjoyed being in it.

The Real Heroes

One fine Sunday morning in the spring of 1937, Mr. Rogers parked the family car in front of the Latrobe Presbyterian Church, a large, redbrick Romanesque building with a tall bell tower, located at 428 Main Street. Mrs. Rogers, holding Freddie's hand, climbed out and hurried toward a side door that would lead them to Reverend McKee's study.

Just as Mrs. Rogers raised her hand to knock, the door opened, and Reverend McKee stepped out.

"Well, good morning, Mrs. Rogers! And good morning to you, too, Freddie," Reverend McKee said. "I was just on my way to talk to the members of the Mission Committee, but I'm sure they won't mind waiting if you need to discuss a matter with me."

"Freddie and I just came by to invite you and Mrs. McKee to dinner after the service," Mrs. Rogers said. "Ruth is cooking a pot roast, and we'd be so pleased if you could join us."

"Oh, you know we could never turn down an invitation to dine on one of Ruth's excellent meals and to enjoy the company that goes with it," Reverend McKee said. "I'll accept for both me and my wife."

"Wonderful!" Mrs. Rogers said. "I'll see Mrs. McKee in Sunday school and let her know that I've talked to you."

"Well, she's playing the organ for this morning's service because Roberta has a bad cold," Reverend McKee said, "so she'll probably be in the sanctuary practicing the hymns since this was a last-minute request. I'll let her know. She'll be delighted too."

"Then we'll expect you and Mrs. McKee as soon after the service as you can get there," Mrs. Rogers said.

When his Sunday school class was over, Freddie met his parents and his McFeely grandparents in the sanctuary and sat in the middle of the pew, between his mother and his grandfather, which is what he always enjoyed doing. It made him feel very safe.

As Freddie listened to the organ prelude, he remembered what his Sunday school teacher had just said, that music in church is very important because it is one of the ways we praise the Lord. Freddie had heard all of these songs many times before, but he never got tired of them. It was hard for him to explain how music made him feel—there was a peace inside him for which he could find no words to describe.

During the service, when the congregation sang hymns, Freddie sang out in his strongest voice.

When Reverend McKee began his sermon, Freddie paid very close attention. He knew that some of the young people used this time to draw pictures on the back of the church bulletin or to pass notes to one another, but Freddie wanted to hear every word the minister had to say.

Freddie thought Reverend McKee said such wonderful things. At school, several of the students in his class talked about how their heroes were Dick Tracy or Buck Rogers from the Saturday-morning serials at the movie theaters in downtown Latrobe. But Freddie never thought of them as heroes. To him, Reverend McKee, the man who stood in the pulpit of this church every Sunday morning, was a real hero. Freddie wanted to be like him. Once, when he mentioned this to his parents, they told him that men who decided to become ministers went to seminary after college. That was one of the things Freddie thought he wanted to do.

Reverend McKee's message today was about forgiving people who did wrong things to others. "It is sometimes easier to forgive our enemies than our friends," he said. "Often, the hardest thing to do is to forgive the people we love."

Freddie had never heard anyone say that before. He thought the only people who did mean things were your enemies, but what if someone he knew and loved did something he thought was wrong? What would he do? he wondered. It was something he would ask Reverend McKee.

"I enjoyed your sermon very much, Reverend McKee," Mr. Rogers said at dinner. "You always say something that will guide me through the rest of the week."

"I'm delighted to hear that, Mr. Rogers," Reverend McKee said. "I always hope that will be the end result of the meager words I choose."

When the table conversation suddenly turned to Ruth's wonderful dinner, Freddie realized that if he didn't ask his question now, he might not be able to, so when there was a momentary lull in the conversation, he said, "Reverend McKee, did someone you love ever do something to you that you couldn't forgive?"

Reverend McKee finished chewing his meat, wiped his mouth with his napkin, and said, "I am always quite impressed, Freddie, when I realize that a young person was actually listening to my sermon." He smiled. "Yes, I forgave a friend of mine in college for doing something that I thought no friend would ever do to me. It wasn't easy. I had to pray about it a lot. We just don't expect family or friends to do mean things to us, so when they do, it's very difficult to deal with."

Mrs. Rogers looked at Freddie. "Has someone done something to upset you, Freddie?" she asked.

"Oh, no, Mama," Freddie replied. "That's never happened to me, but I wasn't sure what I should do if it did."

"You'd probably feel very bad, Freddie," Reverend McKee said, "and you'd probably lose a lot of sleep over it. But if you pray really hard, the Lord will show you the true Christian way."

"I understand," Freddie said.

For the rest of that Sunday, Freddie thought about all of the wonderful things he had heard during the day from Reverend McKee. Right before he went to sleep that night, he decided that when he grew up, he wanted people to feel the same way about what he said to them too.

Difficult Decisions

"Nana will be here in a few minutes, Freddie," Mrs. Rogers said. "She has a new piece for the piano that she wants you to learn."

Freddie wondered what it could be. He knew that whenever his McFeely grandparents went to Pittsburgh, his grandmother always stopped at one of the city's biggest music shops to buy him sheet music.

Just last month, Grandmother McFeely had brought back his own book of Presbyterian hymns. "Always remember the first verse of the ninety-fifth Psalm, Freddie," she told him. "Come, let us sing for joy to the Lord." She turned to page forty-seven in the hymnal. "This is the hymn I want you to practice first. 'Come, Christians, Join to Sing.'"

Freddie studied the notes for a few minutes, then he put his hands on the keys of the organ and began to play.

To his surprise, Grandmother McFeely started singing, "Come, Christians, join to sing. Alleluia! Amen!"

Now, Mrs. Rogers added her voice with "Loud praise to Christ our King. Alleluia! Amen!"

Freddie had never before played the organ and sung at the same time, but he felt such a stirring inside him that he joined in with, "Let all, with heart and voice, before His throne rejoice. Praise is His gracious choice. Alleluia! Amen!"

"Oh, Freddie that was absolutely wonderful," Grandmother McFeely had said. "That is one of my favorite hymns."

Over the next couple of months, Freddie eagerly made his way through the *Presbyterian Hymnal*. Now, it had become almost a tradition for whatever members of the family were in the Rogers' home at the time to gather around the organ and sing hymns.

Just then, the front door opened, bringing Freddie back to the present.

"Hi, Nana!" Freddie said. "What's my surprise?"

Grandmother McFeely pulled a piece of sheet music out of a paper bag and showed it to him. "Paderewski's Minuet in G!" she said.

"Oh, Nana! Everyone talks about how hard that is," Freddie said. "Do you really think I can learn to play it?"

"Of course I do," Grandmother McFeely said. "I also have another surprise for you. I talked to Edwina Byrne, whom I consider the best piano teacher in Pittsburgh, and she has agreed to stop by your house when she's in town to hear you play."

Freddie blinked. "Really?" he gasped.

Just then, Mrs. Rogers came in from the kitchen with a tea service. "Now, what are you two conspiring about?" she asked.

Freddie quickly told her.

"Oh, Mother! How wonderful!" Mrs. Rogers said.

"And the piece I'd like for you to play for Edwina, Freddie, is Paderewski's Minuet in G, because it is now the goal of every child taking piano lessons," Grandmother McFeely said. "It's considered a mark of achievement, but it's really written in a style that Mozart used, and since you've already mastered several of Mozart's sonatas, I don't think it will be difficult to learn."

"I'll do it, Grandma," Freddie said. "I'll start right now."

✿ ✿ ✿ ✿

After school, for the next week, Freddie did almost nothing else but practice Paderewski's Minuet in G. Then, on Saturday, his grandmother McFeely called to say that Edwina Byrne was in town for a few hours and wanted to listen to Freddie play. Freddie thought he was ready.

"We'll be right over, darling," Grandmother McFeely said.

Freddie began pacing back and forth in the parlor. Once, he had a coughing spell, which he thought might turn the day into a disaster, but he took his medicine and several deep breaths, and by the time his grandmother arrived with Miss Byrne, Freddie felt he had himself under control.

Edwina Byrne seemed more like a favorite aunt than a stern piano teacher. "Freddie, I've been looking forward to this day," she said. "Let me hear you play your favorite piece."

"I have a lot of favorite pieces, Miss Byrne," Freddie said, "but I've been working hard on Paderewski's Minuet in G, and I'd like to play that for you."

Miss Byrne raised an eyebrow. "My goodness, Freddie, that is quite an achievement," she said. "I heard Paderewski play his minuet in Paris a few years ago," she told Mrs. Rogers and Grandmother McFeely. She turned back to Freddie and, with a twinkle in her eye, added, "I'm going to close my eyes and see if I can tell the difference."

Freddie swallowed hard. "I'll try to make it sound the same," he said.

He turned around and looked at the keyboard. He closed his eyes too, for just a moment, trying to remember how the minuet had sounded when he had heard it on the radio.

Then Freddie began playing.

Within seconds, he felt as though his fingers had taken on lives of their own. They were dancing over the keys as if he had no control over them. When he finished, he sat

perfectly still for just a few seconds, then he stood up and turned around.

Miss Byrne's head was bowed, and her eyes were still closed. Freddie held his breath.

All of a sudden a smile began to form on Miss Byrne's face, but she didn't open her eyes. Instead, she said, "Mr. Paderewski, it is such an honor to hear you play your Minuet in G."

Freddie couldn't believe his ears.

Mrs. Rogers and Grandmother McFeely broke into applause.

Freddie bowed deeply. "Thank you very much," he said.

Miss Byrne stood up. "I shall be happy to work with Freddie when I'm in Latrobe," she said. "In fact, I'm looking forward to learning some things from him, too."

Now, more than ever before, Freddie was confused. He still thought about becoming a minister, but when he listened to concerts on the radio, he wanted to become a musician.

By the next Sunday morning, Freddie was so frustrated about what he wanted to accomplish in his life, he could hardly get ready for Sunday school. He felt as though he were standing on a street corner and he didn't know in which direction to go. He kept looking down each street to see where it led, but everything was hazy, as if the entire world were covered with fog.

Finally, Freddie managed to get his clothes on, but only after his parents had checked on him several times and kept asking him if he was sick.

"I feel fine," he said, but he coughed twice and sneezed three times as he said it.

Freddie made it through Sunday school, but only by sitting at the back of the room so he wouldn't have to talk to anyone.

When Freddie got to the sanctuary, he

found his parents and his grandparents in their usual pew. He took his seat between his mother and Grandfather McFeely, but he didn't say much to either one of them. He did notice, though, that his mother and his grandmother exchanged worried looks. How could he explain his confusion if he didn't understand it himself?

When the service began, the hymns seemed off-key, as if the organist kept missing notes, and Freddie found himself only mumbling the words. Then Reverend McKee rose to preach his sermon on what he called "inner discipline."

Freddie had heard his parents use the word "discipline" before, but they were always talking about discipline or lack of discipline in children: those who did or did not mind their parents. Freddie knew the word "inner" meant inside, so how would parents know their children were acting right if they couldn't *see* what they did? he wondered.

He leaned forward to make sure he heard every word of Reverend McKee's explanation.

"I think a successful person is one who realizes what he *can't* do," Reverend McKee began.

Freddie had never before heard anyone say that you couldn't do anything you set your mind to.

"When we finally resign ourselves to the wishes that will never come true," Reverend McKee continued, "we'll discover that there will be enormous energies available within us for whatever we *can* do."

Although Freddie heard the rest of the sermon, it was those beginning sentences that lingered with him long after he and his family left the church.

For the first time in weeks, his head no longer felt as though it was a jumble of decisions he had to make. Freddie now knew that all human beings should do the best they can, as much as they can, but that they should understand that they will probably never be able to do everything they *wished* they could do.

The Brick Factory

One morning in 1938, when Freddie had been home sick from school for several days, he woke up and started thinking about bricks. He wasn't exactly sure why, although it could have been because the week before, Miss Tomb, his teacher, had asked everyone in the class to tell what their fathers did for a living. Freddie realized that he had only a vague idea as to what his father's job really was.

"He's the president of the McFeely Brick Company," Freddie said. "It's his job to see that the bricks get made right."

"How does he do that?" John Cunningham asked him.

"I don't know," Freddie said.

"Well, does he just sit in his office and tell people what to do, or does he actually make the bricks?" another student asked.

"I don't know," Freddie repeated.

Everyone else in the class seemed to know more about what their fathers did for a living than he did. In fact, several of the boys said they would be taking over their fathers' businesses when they finished college.

Freddie had never thought about doing that. But from what he was hearing now, this was what boys were expected to do. Freddie had talked to his parents a lot about becoming a minister or a musician. But he had never talked to them about working at the McFeely Brick Company so that he could eventually become the president, like his father.

Freddie sat up and took a deep breath. He

coughed a couple of times, but he didn't lie back down. Instead, he got out of bed and started pacing around the room.

Were his parents and grandparents disappointed in him? he wondered. Did they secretly wish that he were more interested in bricks than in sermons or music?

Suddenly, Freddie stopped pacing and got back into bed. He now knew exactly what he was going to do. He would tell his father that if he was going to become president of the McFeely Brick Company one of these days, he needed to know more about bricks. He'd ask his father if he could go with him to work from time to time to see how he ran the company.

When Mr. Rogers got home that evening, Freddie greeted him at the door, gave him a hug and a kiss, and asked him how his day went.

"It was very busy, but we've lined up a couple

of new customers, so I certainly can't complain about anything," Mr. Rogers said. "How was your day? Are you feeling better?"

"Yes, much, much better, and I'm planning to go back to school tomorrow," Freddie said. "Papa, I—"

"Well, I'm glad to hear that, Freddie, because a new Shirley Temple movie opens downtown tonight, *Little Miss Broadway*. I thought if you were feeling better, we'd all go see it. How does that sound?"

"Oh, I'd love it, Papa," Freddie said, "but if you'd rather stay home and tell me how bricks are made, that would be fine too."

Mr. Rogers gave Freddie a puzzled look, then he suddenly laughed. "Now, that's a good joke, Freddie," he said, "but I've seen bricks all day, and I wouldn't mind hearing Shirley Temple sing instead."

"Okay, Papa, but I really do think that I should know how bricks are made," Freddie said. "Last week in school, when I was telling the class about your job, I didn't know the answers to a lot of the questions they asked."

"Oh, so that's what this is all about," Mr. Rogers said. "I'll be happy to take you to the brick factory one of these days when you're feeling up to it, all right?"

Freddie nodded. "All right," he said. He thought it would be better to wait until they were actually there to tell his father that he was going to forget sermons and music so he could become president of the McFeely Brick Company after his father no longer wanted to do the job.

With that decided, Freddie enjoyed *Little Miss Broadway*. He loved the songs, especially "Be Optimistic," "We Should Be Together," and "Swing Me an Old-Fashioned Tune." During the movie, just listening to Shirley Temple sing made him forget that he had decided to give up music.

❖ ❖ ❖ ❖

It was three more weeks before Freddie was able to go with his father to the brick factory. It was a Wednesday, school was out because of a national holiday, and Freddie was feeling well, so everything worked out perfectly.

"Grandfather McFeely will be here this morning, too, Freddie," Mr. Rogers said as he pulled into the parking space reserved for him. "I telephoned him yesterday and told him you wanted to learn all about bricks, so he's going to take you on a tour."

"I haven't seen Ding Dong for a couple of weeks, and I've missed him," Freddie said, "so this will be even more fun."

"Well, your grandfather is thinking about raising cattle," Mr. Rogers said, "so he's been traveling around western Pennsylvania and eastern Ohio, talking to farmers about which breed they think is best for this part of the country."

Grandfather McFeely was waiting in Mr.

Rogers's office when Freddie and his father got there.

"Ding Dong!" Freddie cried, giving his grandfather a big hug. "I've missed you!"

"I've missed you, too, Freddie," Grandfather McFeely said. "I was glad when your father called me and said you wanted to know how bricks are made."

"I thought I should know, since"—Freddie stopped and looked at his father—"since I plan to take over the company when I grow up."

Freddie could tell by the look on his father's face that he hadn't expected to hear that.

"Well, now, that is news," Mr. Rogers finally said. "What happened to your plans to become either a minister or a musician?"

"Oh, I can play the piano or the organ after I get home from the factory, and if I teach Sunday school, then that's almost like being a minister," Freddie said. "Besides, I think it's important for sons to follow in the footsteps of their fathers and grandfathers." He paused, took a deep breath, and added, "I'm the only boy in our family, and I'm supposed to do this."

Grandfather McFeely looked at Mr. Rogers. "Well, James, then I suppose I should show this young man around," he said, "so he can see what it is that we do here during the week."

Mr. Rogers nodded. "I'll wait here, because I need to catch up on some paperwork," he said. "When you've finished, come on back and we'll have a soda pop and let Freddie tell us what he thinks about the brick factory."

Grandfather McFeely and Freddie left Mr. Rogers's office and headed into the part of the building where the bricks were made.

"We don't make the kinds of bricks used to build homes, Freddie," Grandfather McFeely said. "This factory makes silica bricks, which are used mostly for lining steel furnaces."

"Why is it so important for them to have such a high quartz content, Ding Dong?" Freddie asked.

Grandfather McFeely stopped and looked at Freddie. He grinned. "Are you sure you've never been to this factory before?" he said. "That's a very intelligent question."

Freddie returned his grandfather's grin. "I've heard you and Papa talking about that at the dinner table," he said.

"Well, Freddie, it's the quartz in the silica that keeps the bricks from cracking when they're in high heat," Grandfather McFeely explained. "It also makes them resistant to the acids in the coal slag." He stopped and looked at Freddie. "Is this making sense?"

"Sort of," Freddie said.

"Is it as interesting as music or preaching sermons?" Grandfather McFeely asked.

Freddie blushed. "Well, it's a different kind of interest, Ding Dong," he finally said.

"I'm interested in it because it's what you and Papa do."

"Well, just remember, Freddie, that your father and I have many interests," Grandfather McFeely said. "Bricks aren't the only important things in our lives."

"I know," Freddie said.

As Freddie and Grandfather McFeely continued their tour of the brick factory, Freddie learned that the factory had two hundred employees, and that it turned out up to sixty thousand silica bricks a day that were mostly sold to line the blast furnaces of the steel mills in Pennsylvania.

When Freddie noticed some white dust in the air, he asked, "Where's that coming from, Ding Dong?"

"That's silica dust, Freddie, and we try to keep the area as free of it as possible," Grandfather McFeely said. "We're not always successful, so we tell the workers to cover their noses and their mouths, but a lot of

them don't like working that way, so they don't."

"What happens if they breathe it in?" Freddie asked.

"It can cause lung problems," Grandfather McFeely said. Freddie could see the sadness in his eyes. "I know you've heard of black lung disease, Freddie, because there are a lot of coal miners who suffer from it. Some brick plant workers get *white* lung disease. It's called silicosis."

All of a sudden, Freddie started coughing.

"We need to get you some fresh air," Grandfather McFeely said. He opened a side door, and he and Freddie stepped out onto a loading dock. "Over there are the kilns. We have ten of them," Grandfather McFeely continued. "That's where the bricks are cooked!"

Freddie laughed at the thought of bricks cooking.

Grandfather McFeely pointed to a narrow-gauge rail line next to the loading dock. "The ganister—that's the siliceous rock—is brought down from the quarry near the top of the mountain by train," he said. "It's crushed and ground and mired with lime and water, then it's placed in molds to dry for a couple of days. After that, it's baked in a kiln for ten days at 2,700 degrees Fahrenheit. The bricks have to cool for seven days before the workers put them in the storage sheds."

"You must have to use a lot of coal to get the kilns so hot," Freddie said.

"We certainly do, and we have to have a steady supply of it, too. Just about the time we get things running smoothly, John L. Lewis pulls the coal miners out on strike," Grandfather McFeely said, "and then, when we come back and get caught up from where we were behind, the steelworkers go out on strike."

Freddie didn't know what to say. He had never heard either his father or his grandfather talk about how difficult it was to make bricks. He started coughing as some of the silica dust blew in their direction.

"I think we need to go back to your father's office," Grandfather McFeely said. "You've seen everything there is to see about making bricks."

But before they reached Mr. Rogers's office, Grandfather McFeely stopped and said, "Freddie, I'm glad you wanted to come here today. Someday this factory will belong to you whether you actually spend much time here or not, and if you own something, you need to know how it works. But it's also important for you to know that your parents do not expect you to take over this business just because it might be something that other young men are planning to do."

Freddie thought for a minute. "I don't really want to make bricks, Ding Dong," he finally said. "I want to play music or preach sermons."

"Freddie, you should always make your dreams your goals," Grandfather McFeely said. "If you do that, you'll be happy and successful in life."

"That's what I want to do, Ding Dong," Freddie said, "but I don't want anyone to be disappointed in me."

Grandfather McFeely gave him a big hug. "Oh, you'll never have to worry about that, Freddie," he said. "Now, then, your father promised us a soda pop when we finished the tour, and right now, I'm thirsty. How about you?"

"So am I, Ding Dong," Freddie said. "Let's go!"

A New Sister

On Tuesday, March 21, 1939, the day after Freddie's eleventh birthday, his parents said they wanted to talk to him about something very important, so they all went into the parlor and sat down.

"It was always our dream to have two children, a boy and a girl," Mrs. Rogers began, "but right after you were born, Dr. Thomas said that having another child might put my health at risk."

"So how would you feel if we *adopted* a baby girl?" Mr. Rogers asked. "After all, you've been our only child for eleven years, and it would be quite an adjustment for everyone concerned, I think."

"Do you really mean that?" Freddie said. He stood up. "Oh, Mama! Papa! I would be so happy to have a baby sister. I could teach her how to play the piano and the organ, and I could show her how to make puppets, and I could . . ." He stopped. "When is she coming to live with us?"

Freddie's parents started laughing.

"Oh, my goodness, Freddie!" Mrs. Rogers said. "These things take time." She laughed again. "You can't just go pick a baby off a tree like you can an apple!"

But it didn't take as long as anyone thought it would.

Within a week, with Dr. Martin's and Dr. Thomas's assistance, an adoption agency in Pittsburgh that was affiliated with the Presbyterian Church called and said that they had a little girl whom they thought would be perfect for the Rogerses.

The following Saturday, Grandfather and Grandmother McFeely arrived at eight o'clock in their new 1939 DeSoto Town Coupe to take everyone to Pittsburgh.

To Freddie, the trip had never seemed so long. He could hardly wait to see his new baby sister.

"What's her name, Mama?" Freddie asked. It had suddenly occurred to him that no one had mentioned that before.

"Well, last night, your father and I finally decided on Nancy Elaine," his mother said. She smiled and looked at Mr. Rogers, who was riding in the front seat with Grandfather McFeely. "I had begun to think that we wouldn't be able to agree on anything."

"We'll probably called her Lainey," Mr. Rogers said.

Lainey, Freddie thought. He liked that.

Finally, they arrived at the hospital and

met with Dr. Merriman, the doctor who had delivered the baby.

"Your daughter is in perfect health," Dr. Merriman told them. "She has no physical problems whatsoever."

Miss Forrester, who was the head of the orphanage, added, "And we're so happy that she can go directly from the hospital to your home."

Just then, a door opened and a nurse carrying Nancy Elaine came into the room. She handed her to Mrs. Rogers. "Here's your daughter," she said.

Once Lainey was in her new crib back in Latrobe, Grandmother McFeely said, "Well, we need to be running along. I'm having some friends over tonight to discuss what we can do to help some of the women who lost their husbands in the coal mine accident last month."

"I feel so sorry for the children," Mrs.

Rogers said. She was looking at Lainey sleeping in her crib. "They'll have to grow up now without fathers."

"Can I help, too, Nana?" Freddie asked.

Grandmother McFeely smiled at him, then gave him a big hug. "Yes, you can help, Freddie," she said. "Just remember those families in your prayers."

The next morning, when Freddie awakened, he could hear Lainey screaming all the way from her bedroom. At first, he thought something was seriously wrong, so he quickly started getting dressed. But before he had finished, the screaming had stopped. By the time he got to Lainey's bedroom, his mother was sitting in a chair, feeding Lainey her bottle.

At first his mother didn't notice him standing at the door, but when she finally looked up, she said, "Well, at least we know her lungs are good, don't we?"

Freddie grinned and nodded. "I won't

have to worry about oversleeping anymore," he said.

"I don't think any of us will for a while," Mrs. Rogers said.

Over the next few weeks, everyone began to adjust to having a new baby in the house. Freddie could still tell that Lainey was more of a surprise to his parents than they thought she would be.

"I love her to death," Mr. Rogers said one evening, "but I guess I was expecting a female Freddie."

"Well, I feel guilty saying this, James," Mrs. Rogers said, "but I guess I was too."

As the months went by, it became more and more apparent to everyone that Lainey had a mind of her own. Several times, Freddie heard Grandmother McFeely call her "very high-spirited."

When Freddie asked his father what that

meant, Mr. Rogers grinned and said, "Well, that's a nice way of saying that Lainey more or less does what she pleases."

Freddie found that interesting. He knew that he had always been expected to mind. That was simply the way things were done in his family.

One evening, when Lainey was six months old, Freddie came down from his room and found his parents sitting in the parlor, passing a crying Lainey back and forth to each other.

"What's wrong?" Freddie asked.

"Well, your sister doesn't seem interested in anything tonight," Mrs. Rogers said.

Freddie thought his mother looked very tired.

"Do you think we should telephone Dr. Thomas?" Mr. Rogers asked. "She may be coming down with something."

"I honestly don't think she's sick, James," Mrs. Rogers said. "Just two days ago, Dr. Thomas pronounced her fit as a fiddle."

"Is she teething?" Mr. Rogers asked.

Mrs. Rogers shook her head and handed her back to Mr. Rogers.

Lainey continued to cry.

"I have an idea," Freddie said. "I'll be right back."

He hurried up the stairs to his room.

When he came back to the parlor, he had a puppet on each hand.

"Oh, my goodness, Freddie!" Mrs. Rogers exclaimed. "I've never seen those puppets before!"

"They were going to be a surprise for Lainey," Freddie said, "but I was waiting until I had finished making up a story for her." The boy puppet had short black yarn for hair. He had a pink mouth and blue eyes. The girl puppet had long yellow yarn for hair. She had a red mouth and brown eyes. On their heads, they both wore gray crowns. "Ruth helped me pick out the colors," Freddie added.

"What are their names, Freddie?" Mr. Rogers asked. He handed Lainey back to Mrs. Rogers, but that didn't stop her from crying.

"Lord Freddie and Lady Elaine," Freddie said.

Mr. and Mrs. Rogers looked at each other and smiled.

"Well, Freddie, your father and I are at our wits' end, trying to find something that will make Lainey happy, and we've had no luck whatsoever," Mrs. Rogers said. "As her big brother, it's your turn. You may now have the floor."

"Thank you," Freddie said.

He stood in front of his parents and Lainey. With a deep voice for Lord Freddie, he said, "Lady Elaine, you seem very unhappy today. What is the matter?"

With a higher voice for Lady Elaine, he answered, "I just want to tell you how happy I am to be your sister, but I can't find the words."

All of a sudden, Lainey stopped crying.

"You don't have to have words for everything, Lady Elaine," Lord Freddie said. "I can tell what you're thinking by the way you smile."

As if on cue, Lainey gave Freddie a big smile.

For the next few minutes, Freddie told Lainey a story about how happy he and his parents were now that she had come to live with them, and about how glad he was to be her brother.

Just as the story ended, Lainey closed her eyes and went to sleep.

"Well, Freddie, you're amazing," Mr. Rogers said. "You seem to be the only one in this family who can get Lainey to do anything tonight."

Mrs. Rogers stood up. "I'll put her down now," she said. "This is the first time she's closed her eyes all day." She turned to Freddie. "Would you like to help me? If she

119

wakes up, you may need to have another story ready."

"All right, Mama," Freddie said.

As Freddie and his mother started up the stairs to Lainey's bedroom, Freddie thought how wonderful it was to have someone else in the house to listen to all of the stories his puppets had to tell.

Last Winter in Florida

For several years, Freddie had spent the months of January, February, and March in Florida, with his McFeely grandparents, his mother, and, after Lainey's arrival in 1939, his little sister. Grandfather McFeely owned a large house in Winter Park, near the town of Orlando, and also rented a smaller beachfront house about fifty miles away on the Atlantic Ocean.

Although Freddie could never say that he was miserable while he was in Florida, the trips always seemed like a mixed blessing to him. On the one hand, he loved the warmer climate because he could play outside after school, while he knew his friends back in Latrobe were having to shovel several feet of snow from off the sidewalks. But he missed those friends and all the things he knew they were doing at school. Freddie wouldn't see them from shortly after Christmas until the first of April, and that was a time when a lot of important things happened in school. He wanted to be there to share them.

Most of all, though, Freddie missed his father. Often, he would be playing on the beach, having a good time, when suddenly, without notice, he would start thinking about how lonely his father must be without him, Lainey, and his mother. Freddie would lie down on the warm sand, close his eyes, and try to picture what his father was doing at that very moment back in Pennsylvania. The highlight of each week for Freddie was when his mother let him telephone his father back in Latrobe.

Sometimes, if things were going well at the brick factory and Mr. Rogers thought he could be away for a week or two, he would either take the train or drive down to Florida once or twice during the winter to see everyone. There were years, though, when his father never came.

Freddie attended a small school near his grandfather's house in Winter Park. A lot of his classmates were just there for the winter months too, like he was, and they weren't really all that interested in making new friends. The rest were permanent residents, some of them the sons and daughters of nearby Rollins College professors. Since they were together all year round, they had already formed their friendships.

As he did in Latrobe, Freddie created his own world, and with his grandfather McFeely there to talk to him, he was able to get through the three months without being too unhappy.

Late one Saturday afternoon in February, just as Freddie returned to the beachfront house after spending a couple of hours showing Lainey how to build a sand castle, Grandfather McFeely held up a book. "Freddie," he said, "when I took your grandmother to the library this morning, Miss Crosby, one of the librarians, said you might like to read this. Your grandmother checked it out for you."

Freddie took the book. "*The Yearling*, by Marjorie Kinnan Rawlings," he said. "I think I heard one of my teachers mention this book, but I've never read it. Is it supposed to be good?"

"Well, it won the Pulitzer Prize for Fiction in nineteen thirty-nine, and that's a very important award, so I think it probably has some merit," Grandfather McFeely said. "Mrs. Rawlings and her husband live in Cross Creek, which is between Lochloosa Lake and Orange Lake, just south of Gainesville, not too far from here. Miss Crosby said that the

book is set in that area during the late eighteen hundreds. She thought you'd enjoy reading it since it's about a boy your age."

"Thank you, Ding Dong," Freddie said. "I just finished my last book, so I think I'll start this one right now."

"If you like it, then maybe you can tell Mrs. Rawlings in person, because she's going to give a talk at Rollins College next week," Grandfather McFeely said. "I thought I'd take you to hear her."

"Really? I've never seen a real writer before," Freddie said. "I'd like that a lot."

Freddie took a quick shower to wash off all the sand, then he put on a clean shirt and some shorts and went out to the screened-in porch that faced the beach and sat down in his favorite rattan chair to read his book.

Within minutes, Freddie was living with Jody Baxter and his family in the central Florida scrublands of the late 1800s. Even though at first the book was hard to follow because the characters spoke the language of the backwoods people, Freddie was soon thinking the way Jody and his parents talked. He was *living* the book.

Along with Jody and his father, Freddie fought off a pack of starving wolves, wrestled alligators in a swamp, and romped with bear cubs. Soon, though, both Jody and Freddie wanted something else, a pet, with whom they could share their thoughts and the corn pone that Mrs. Baxter made.

Looking up from the book for a few minutes, Freddie thought about Mitzi, the family dog, back in Latrobe. She was always ready to sit and listen to him tell her whatever was on his mind. He knew exactly why Jody needed a pet too.

"Freddie!" Mrs. Rogers called. "It's time to eat."

Freddie marked his place in the book, then went into the dining room, where the rest of the family was already seated.

"I really like *The Yearling,* Nana," Freddie said. "Thank you so much for getting it for me."

"You're welcome, Freddie," Grandmother McFeely said. "I'll tell Miss Crosby. She'll be pleased, I'm sure."

While they ate, Freddie told everyone what had happened in the book so far. He once began a sentence with "Jody and I are going . . . ," then he stopped, grinned, and said, "I really do believe that I'm living in that cabin with him!"

"That's the sign of a good writer, Freddie," Mrs. Rogers said. "You get so caught up in the story, you believe you're actually living it."

"I'm going to take Freddie to hear Mrs. Rawlings next week," Grandfather McFeely said. "She's giving a talk at Rollins Collge."

"Oh, that is wonderful," Grandmother McFeely said. "This is something you can tell

129

your classmates about when you get back to Latrobe."

Freddie hadn't really thought about that, but he decided it was a very good idea.

After dinner, Freddie returned to *The Yearling*. When Jody's father was bitten on the arm by a rattlesnake, he quickly found a doe to kill so he could use its heart to remove the poison from his wound. Jody discovered that the doe had a fawn, and he convinced his father to allow him to keep it.

It was after midnight when Freddie finally finished the book, but he couldn't immediately go to sleep because he kept thinking about all of the things that had happened to Jody. He knew that Jody wasn't real, but Mrs. Rawlings had made him seem so real that Freddie felt as though he were a new best friend. How could a writer do this? Freddie wondered. How could a writer put together words that would make people *believe* what they were reading was real? He knew that this was one of the things he wanted to do too. He'd ask Mrs. Rawlings for her secret.

On Wednesday evening of the following week, Freddie and his grandfather McFeely drove the five blocks to the lecture hall on the campus of Rollins College, where Marjorie Kennan Rawlings was going to speak.

"Rollins College is one of the best schools in the country, Freddie," Grandfather McFeely said. "If you went here, we'd get to see each other when the family comes down for the winter."

"I know, Ding Dong, and I've thought about it a lot," Freddie said, "but I sort of have my heart set on going to Dartmouth."

"The Ivy League is outstanding, of course, but here at Rollins, President Holt has really created a wonderful atmosphere for learning," Grandfather McFeely said. "They stress individualization in education, which means that the students and the teachers work closely together. You don't find that at a lot of colleges. It's easy to get lost."

"Well, I'm not even in high school yet, Ding Dong," Freddie said, "so I've still got time to think about it."

The lecture hall was crowded, but Freddie and his grandfather found two seats together near the front of the room.

"Can you see all right?" Grandfather McFeely whispered.

Freddie nodded. "Thank you for bringing me to this," he whispered back. "I hope Mrs. Rawlings lets us ask questions."

"She probably will," Grandfather McFeely said.

President Holt introduced Marjorie Kennan Rawlings as a friend of the state of Florida and a friend of Rollins College. He told how she had sold a story called "Cracker Chidlings" to *Scribner's Magazine* in 1931, how it had come to the attention of the famous editor Maxwell Perkins, and that the rest was history.

Mrs. Rawlings walked to the front of the room, thanked President Holt, and began to tell the audience about how she had come to live at Cross Creek.

"It's not just a place where I write, it's a place where I immerse myself in my surroundings and learn about every plant, shrub, tree, and flower," she explained.

"When my husband and I first moved there, I cooked three meals a day on a wood-burning stove, and I washed clothes in an iron pot. We lived like our neighbors.

"At first, they were wary of us, but then they opened up their lives and experiences to me.

"I took notes. I took lots of notes. So many notes, in fact, that I filled almost a hundred notebooks.

"But in the end, I was also living what I was writing about."

Freddie listened closely to the rest of what Mrs. Rawlings was saying, which was mostly about the new book she was working on, *Cross Creek*, but when it came time for the question-and-answer session, Freddie didn't raise his hand because his only question had already been answered. Mrs. Rawlings and her husband had lived exactly the way that Jody and his parents had lived in *The Yearling*. But did that mean a person could never write about something he had not experienced?

Suddenly, Freddie raised his hand. He had to know the answer to *that* question.

Mrs. Rawlings acknowledged him. "Yes, young man?" she said.

"I want to write too, Mrs. Rawlings, but I don't think I can do everything that I want to write about," Freddie said. "Does this mean I can't be a writer?"

"That is an excellent question," Mrs. Rawlings said. "I don't think that *The Yearling* would have been as successful if my husband and I hadn't moved to Cross Creek. But what I did is only one type of writing. A lot of writers experience their novels in their heads, and so can you. You can write about what you *see* in your mind, but in some way, remember, everything we come in contact with influences what we put down on paper." She smiled. "Does that make sense?"

Freddie nodded. "I think so," he said. "Thank you."

When the lecture was over, Grandfather McFeely asked Freddie if he wanted to meet Mrs. Rawlings, but there was such a long line of people waiting to talk to her that Freddie said no.

"I'm glad I came, though, Ding Dong," Freddie said, "because now when I read a book, I'll have a better understanding of how the writer put the words on paper."

"How about an ice-cream cone before we

head back to the house?" Grandfather McFeely asked.

Freddie laughed. "I love to tell my friends back in Latrobe about how we buy ice-cream cones in February and then walk down the street licking them," he said. "They can't believe it."

All during March, Freddie tried to come to terms with some changes he was beginning to experience within himself. He'd be in high school soon, something he was actually looking forward to because of the new directions it would lead him. But he had to wrestle with a decision he knew he had to make, a decision that would probably upset the entire family. Still, Freddie knew that it was the right thing to do, and that, eventually, his family would understand.

Grandfather McFeely came into the kitchen and said, "Well, I took the trunks to the

Railway Express Office, so they should be back in Latrobe in four days, and the car's packed, so all we need to do is get inside and head north to Pennsylvania."

It was the last day of March, and the three months in Florida were at an end.

"I'm forgetting to do something," Grandmother McFeely said. "I just know I am."

"Mother, we go through this every year," Mrs. Rogers said. "The Johnsons have the keys to the house, and they've been taking care of it for years, so there's nothing to worry about."

"Well, I guess you're right, Nancy," Grandmother McFeely said. "It's just that something feels different, that's all."

Freddie swallowed hard. Was his grandmother reading his mind? he wondered. He swallowed hard again and said, "I don't want to come here next winter. I want to stay in Latrobe."

For just a minute, there was stunned

silence, then Mrs. Rogers said, "I don't understand, Freddie. What do you mean?"

Freddie gave them the speech he had been rehearsing almost since they had arrived in January.

"It's hard to leave my friends at school, and it's hard to leave Papa. I love being with everyone here, but I don't think I can do this anymore and have any kind of a life in high school. There's just too much going on, and I don't want to miss any of it."

When Mrs. Rogers didn't say anything, Grandfather McFeely said, "You see, Nancy, as hard as it is for parents to accept, children do eventually grow up, and, well, that's what's happening to Freddie. He's no longer a child. He's becoming a young man."

The Magic of Buttermilk Falls

In 1931, Grandfather McFeely bought a forty-eight-acre farm in the woodlands of Indiana County, northeast of Latrobe. At the eastern end was a forty-five-foot waterfall, called Buttermilk Falls because a Mrs. Wilson, who lived in a house below the falls, was famous for making buttermilk. After Grandfather McFeely bought the property, everyone in the family referred to the farm as Buttermilk Falls.

During the Depression, Grandfather McFeely hired local residents to build a large house with stone fences and decks around it, horse stables, and a three-car garage. Two small dams were constructed just upstream from the falls. One pond was for swimming, and the other pond was for goldfish.

Over the years, Freddie and his family would often drive up on a Sunday afternoon to have dinner with the McFeely grandparents. During the summer, Freddie would spend weeks at a time on the farm.

To Freddie, Buttermilk Falls was a magical place, one that seemed, more than any other place he ever was, to stimulate his imagination and allow him to think of all kinds of stories his puppets could act out.

Normally, Freddie never invited anyone else to come with him to Buttermilk Falls. But in the summer of 1942, with World War II raging in Europe and the Pacific, he met a boy his age from Lubbock, Texas. Clay Henry had come to Latrobe with his mother to live with his grandparents while his father was at war.

Unlike most of the rest of Freddie's friends in Latrobe, Clay was very interested in Freddie's puppets, and he would sit and listen for hours on end to all of the stories that they had to tell.

Clay had asthma, so his mother never wanted him to go too far from his grandmother's house. Mrs. Rogers, seeing how much Freddie enjoyed being with Clay, finally convinced Mrs. Henry that she would be able to recognize the signs of an approaching asthma attack and would make sure that Clay was taken care of. That seemed to satisfy Mrs. Henry. As long as Clay was at Freddie's house, she wasn't worried about him, she told Mrs. Rogers. So when Freddie suggested to his parents that Clay accompany them to Buttermilk Falls the next Sunday, they agreed that it was a good idea.

On the trip up from Latrobe, Lainey sat in the middle of the backseat, between Clay and Freddie, and Freddie entertained her with puppets.

After Lainey fell asleep, Mrs. Rogers turned around and whispered, "Clay, Freddie is about the only one in this family Lainey will sit still for." She chuckled softly. "She's a handful, I can tell you, and I was afraid that she'd pester you."

"Well, Freddie not only entertained Lainey, but he entertained me, too, Mrs. Rogers," Clay said. He chuckled. "My mother told me to behave, so I was glad to have Freddie along to keep me busy."

When Mr. Rogers pulled their automobile into the drive in front of the house, Grandfather and Grandmother McFeely were standing there to greet them. They were delighted to have Clay as their guest, they told him.

"I'm sure Freddie has plans for you, Clay,"

Grandfather McFeely said, "so we'll not keep you boys here."

"Thank you, Mr. McFeely," Clay said.

The first thing Freddie did was show Clay around the house.

"It's like a hotel," Clay said. "I've never seen a house this big before."

"It is kind of like a hotel, because Grandfather is always having people stay here," Freddie said. "He likes to entertain a lot."

"Is that Buttermilk Falls?" Clay asked. He was pointing to a big picture hanging over the huge fireplace.

Freddie nodded. "It's a photograph that was taken in nineteen thirty, before Ding Dong bought the farm," he said, "but it really hasn't changed all that much, as you'll see."

From the living room, Freddie took Clay to the huge kitchen and introduced him to Mr. and Mrs. Wesenberg.

The Wesenbergs shook hands with Clay.

"Mrs. Wesenberg takes care of the house

both when the family is here, and when it isn't, and she cooks all of the wonderful meals we eat," Freddie said. "Are we going to eat on the porch this afternoon?" he asked Mrs. Wesenberg.

"Yes, we are," Mrs. Wesenberg replied. "Would you boys like to help Mr. Wesenberg finish setting the tables?"

"Sure!" Freddie said.

He and Clay each picked up several plates and took them out to the back porch, which ran the full length of the house and overlooked Buttermilk Falls.

"Isn't it beautiful?" Freddie said as he and Clay began to set the plates on the table. "I could stay here forever, really I could, Clay."

"I think I could, too, Freddie," Clay said.

When Freddie and Clay had finished helping the Wesenbergs, Freddie said, "I want to show you how I can walk the stone fences. Come on!"

Freddie jumped up on the stone ledge that

ran along the back porch. When Clay didn't immediately follow, Freddie jumped down and said, "What's wrong?"

"That looks dangerous," Clay said.

"It's not, really," Freddie said. He jumped back on the ledge again. "My mother and my grandmother used to get so upset with me because I loved to walk on top of these ledges and fences all over the farm. They were always telling me to get down, but then one day Ding Dong said, 'Let the kid climb on the walls! He's got to learn to do things for himself!'"

"He really said that?" Clay said.

Freddie nodded. "Well, when I heard him, I couldn't believe it," he said, "because my mother, and my grandmother, too, were always afraid that I was going to get scratched up or break a bone or something."

"I wish I had somebody to say something like that for me, Freddie," Clay said. "My mother is always afraid that I'm going to break an arm or a leg too, if I'm climbing the trees in my grandparents' backyard."

Freddie grinned. "All right, Clay Henry, I'm telling you now," he said. "You get up on this ledge and start following me!"

When Clay didn't move, Freddie jumped down off the wall, pulled off his shoe, took off his sock, stuck his hand in it, and said, using a different voice, "It's all about *freedom*, Clay Henry! The freedom to be yourself. That's what it's all about."

Clay started laughing.

"You're a kid, and you have to act like a kid," Freddie the puppet continued.

"My mother doesn't think a fourteen-year-old boy is a kid," Clay countered.

"Well, if you weren't allowed to act like a kid when you were a kid, then you have to make up for lost time," Freddie the puppet said. "You have to have some time to *be* yourself instead of just always *behaving* yourself!"

Clay thought for a minute. "Hmm. That makes a lot of sense," Clay said to the puppet. "You're very intelligent for a sock."

Freddie started giggling. "You're not supposed to think of me as a sock," he said. "You're supposed to think of me as someone who can help you solve your problems."

"Sorry," Clay said. He thought for a minute. "Well, I've made a decision," he said to the puppet. "I'm going to take your advice!"

Freddie took the sock off his hand, put it on his foot, put his shoe back on, and said, "These walls are like rock highways, Clay. They go all over the farm. You'll love it."

For the next hour, Freddie and Clay crisscrossed the farm, never once getting off the stone fences.

Once, when they got close to the house, Mrs. Rogers waved at them. Freddie was sure that his mother was almost ready to ask if Freddie thought Clay should be doing that, but she didn't, which Freddie appreciated.

Freddie and Clay had just climbed down from one of the fences to look at the shuffleboard court when they heard Mrs. Wesenberg ringing the bell to call the family to lunch.

"After we eat, we'll go to the falls," Freddie said. "I brought two bathing suits."

"That's what I've really been looking forward to," Clay admitted. "I can hardly wait."

When the meal was over and Freddie and Clay had been dismissed, they changed into their swimming suits and headed for the waterfall.

When they reached it, Freddie said, "I have a surprise for you, Clay. I didn't want to tell you about it until we got here. Follow me."

With Clay behind him, Freddie began climbing down the steep embankment over which the falls cascaded. When they were about halfway down, Freddie pointed to a rocky ledge that disappeared behind the water.

"You can go *behind* the falls," Freddie said. "Not a lot of people know that."

"Oh, this is really great," Clay said.

"But you have to be careful," Freddie said, "because the ledge is slippery."

Freddie and Clay slowly made their way along the ledge until they were totally hidden by the falling water.

"I love the sound of a waterfall," Clay said. "I wish I could listen to it at night, because I think it would help me go to sleep."

"It *is* peaceful, isn't it?" Freddie said.

"It sure is," Clay said. "I could stay here forever."

Freddie turned to him. "I know you worry about your father," he said. "I just wanted to tell you that we mention him in our prayers every night."

"Thank you," Clay said. "It's hard for me to talk about sometimes."

"There are a lot of things that are hard to talk about, aren't there?" Freddie said.

Clay nodded. "There sure are," he agreed.

"Sometimes I get so confused about what I want to do when I grow up, because I like so many things," Freddie said. "Whatever I finally decide to do, whether I become a musician or a minister or something else, I just hope that I'll be able to help people solve their problems."

"Well, I think you'd be really good at that, Freddie," Clay said, "because I already feel better about myself and all that's happened to me since I met you."

For the next several minutes, Freddie and Clay sat quietly on the ledge, letting the falling water cascade over their outstretched legs. Suddenly Freddie said, "I'm thirsty!"

"Can we drink this water?" Clay asked.

"Grandfather McFeely says we probably shouldn't," Freddie said. "But there's a springhouse just up the hill, and it has the best water in the world."

Freddie and Clay stood up carefully and made their way back to the edge of the embankment.

When they reached the springhouse, Freddie pumped some water into the tin cup that was attached to the pump handle with a chain. "Try it," he said to Clay.

Clay took a long drink. "It's so sweet!" he said. "It's delicious!"

"I know," Freddie said. He pumped some more water into the tin cup and drank it all. "I wish the water in Latrobe tasted this good."

As they started back to the house, Freddie said, "Let's go horseback riding! I'll get Mr. Wesenberg to saddle up old Sally for you, and he can saddle up Mary for me."

"Is Sally gentle?" Clay asked. "I've never been on a horse before."

Freddie stopped and stared at him.

"You're from West Texas, and you've never been on a horse before?" he said. "That's incredible!"

Clay gave him a big grin and said, "You're from western Pennsylvania, and you've never been down in a coal mine before? That's incredible!"

For a couple of minutes, Freddie didn't say anything, then he grinned back at Clay and said, "You're quick, and I should have known better than to say that. People don't think when they say things like that, do they?"

"No, they don't," Clay said. "When we first got to Latrobe, Grandmother's friends kept asking me where my boots and ten-gallon hat were."

"*Really?*" Freddie said.

Clay nodded. "I guess people here think that everybody from Texas is a cowboy," he said, "but I've never been to a rodeo in my entire life."

"You're right, Clay, and people really

shouldn't do that," Freddie said. "I guess people in Texas think we're all coal miners up here."

Clay nodded again. "When I told my teacher that I was moving to southwestern Pennsylvania, she told me that whatever I did, I should never become a coal miner, because I'd die of black lung disease."

When Freddie and Clay reached the house, the warm air had already dried their bathing suits, so they changed quickly into some old clothes that Freddie kept at the house to wear when he went horseback riding.

After they were dressed, Mrs. Wesenberg told them that Mr. Wesenberg was already at the stables because he thought they might want to go riding after they came in from playing at the waterfall.

Sally and Mary were already saddled and waiting when Freddie and Clay got to the stables, so for the next two hours they rode over almost the entire farm.

Finally, Freddie said, "I think the horses

are getting tired, so maybe we'd better take them back to the stable. They're not as young as they used to be."

"It's kind of funny that I had to come all the way to Pennsylvania to ride a horse," Clay said. "You just never know what's going to happen to you in your life, do you?"

Freddie shook his head. "No, you don't," he said, "but I guess you need to be prepared for whatever it is."

Just then, Freddie heard Mrs. Wesenberg's bell, and all of a sudden he had the strangest feeling that what was going to happen in the next few minutes would be very difficult for everyone.

"What's that for?" Clay asked.

"I think we need to go back to the house," Freddie said. "When the bell rings like that, it's usually because somebody has something important to tell us."

Freddie thought he caught just a glint of fear in Clay's eyes.

Sally and Mary knew they were heading back to the stable, so neither Freddie nor Clay had to do much other than just stay in the saddle.

Mr. Wesenberg was waiting for them, and Freddie could see that he had a strained look on his face. Usually, Freddie would help Mr. Wesenberg unsaddle whatever horse he had ridden, then help feed her. This time, before Freddie could even offer, Mr. Wesenberg said, "You boys need to head on to the house."

Neither Freddie nor Clay said anything as they started up the path. Just as they reached the back porch, Grandfather McFeely stepped outside.

He put his arms around both Clay's and Freddie's shoulders. "Your mother just telephoned, Clay," he said gently. "I hate to have to tell you this, son, but your father has been reported killed in action in the Pacific."

Freddie heard Clay gasp, and he felt his

grandfather's arms squeeze him tighter.

"I'm sorry, son. There aren't a lot of words that a person can think of to say at a time like this," Grandfather McFeely said, "but I have no doubt that your father was a very brave man and that in giving his life for this country he was helping to preserve the freedoms we hold so dearly."

"Yes, sir," Clay managed to say.

"Mrs. Rogers told your mother that just as soon as we could get everyone together, we'd be heading back to Latrobe," Grandfather McFeely said.

Clay wiped a tear off his cheek and looked up at Mr. McFeely. "Do you mind if I'm alone with Freddie for just a minute, sir, before we start back?" he asked.

"No, of course not, son," Grandfather McFeely said. "You stay out here as long as you want to."

When Grandfather McFeely had left, Clay sat down on the ground, picked up a stick, and started making lines in the dirt. After a few minutes, he looked up at Freddie and said, "Will you tell me again what your grandfather McFeely told you that summer just before you left to go back home to Latrobe?"

Freddie took a deep breath. "He said, 'Freddie, you made this day a really special day for me, just by being yourself. There's only one person in the world like you. And I happen to like you just the way you are.'"

Now, tears were streaming down Clay's face. "Right before my father left to go to war, he and I went fishing," he said. "We had never done anything like that together before, and it was one of the best days of my life." Clay took a handkerchief out of his pocket and blew his nose. "He never talked to me a lot, and there were times when I thought he wished he had a son who liked the same things he did. But on that day, he really seemed to enjoy just being with me." Clay looked directly at Freddie. "Tell me the truth. Do you think my father felt the same way about me that your grandfather feels about you?"

"I don't even have to think about that, Clay," Freddie said without batting an eye. "I know he did."

A Changing World

From time to time, Freddie still had to miss school because of his hay fever or because of complications associated with it. But for the most part, he didn't seem to have as many health problems now that he was in high school as he did when he was in elementary school.

Freddie had never regretted telling his parents and his grandparents that he couldn't spend three months out of the year in Florida anymore. Now he was able to be actively involved in school activities. As president of the Student Council, he had to interact with all the other students, something he wasn't used to. Although this made him a little uncomfortable, he honestly believed that he was doing a good job and that his decisions had made Latrobe High School a better place to be.

When the faculty adviser to the student newspaper, Mr. Hawkins, approached Freddie about being the editor, he jumped at the chance.

"I've always wanted to write," Freddie told him. "I also have an opinion about most things."

"Well, those are good qualities for an editor to have, Freddie," Mr. Hawkins said. "Besides that, you have a knack for getting along with everyone. People respect you and appreciate what you have to say."

With Freddie as editor, more students started reading the newspaper. Sometimes Freddie and Mr. Hawkins had long discussions about some of the stories that Freddie wanted to run.

"We're living in a very sensitive time," Mr. Hawkins told him one day. "You just have to be very careful about certain things."

Freddie understood. But if there was something he honestly thought the students at Latrobe High School needed to think about, he wrote an editorial on it. Although occasionally some of the students and even some of the teachers would tell him they didn't really share his viewpoint, Freddie never angered anyone, because everyone who read what he had written could tell that he had given the matter a lot of thought and that he was writing from his heart.

The two most important issues of the time were labor problems, especially in the coal mines, and the war.

The Allies had already invaded Europe, and the Nazis were retreating. Every morning, Freddie read the Latrobe and Pittsburgh newspapers with his father, trying to find out what had happened in Europe and in the

Pacific the night before. In the evenings, Freddie joined his parents as they huddled around the radio, listening to what had happened during the day.

If that had been Freddie's only contact with the war, it might have seemed like a distant event, but St. Vincent College was located right outside Latrobe, and one of the dormitories had been taken over by the Army Air Corps for a training camp.

One morning, as Freddie was leaving for school, Mrs. Rogers said, "We've invited a couple of the cadets for dinner tonight, so you'll need to make sure you're here to help us entertain them."

"Oh, I wouldn't miss it, Mama!" Freddie said. "Talking to them is better than reading a newspaper or listening to the radio."

Aside from the fact that Freddie knew how much the cadets appreciated having home-cooked meals after subsisting on cafeteria food for weeks, every one of the cadets had told his family how special their time was with the Rogerses because it was just like being back with their own parents.

That always brought tears to Mrs. Rogers's eyes. Freddie and his parents knew that most of these cadets would soon be sent off to fight and that some of them would never return.

"If we can give these young men memories that will sustain them in the difficult times to come," Mrs. Rogers would say, "then let this be part of our war effort."

Nineteen forty-five was a year of tragedy and then triumph for the United States.

On April 12, President Franklin D. Roosevelt died in Warm Springs, Georgia, and Harry S. Truman became the thirty-third president.

President Roosevelt had been a larger than life figure to most Americans because he and his policies were credited with bringing the country out of the depths of the

Great Depression of the 1930s. His death sent most Americans, including Freddie's parents and grandparents, into mourning.

But less than a month later, this grief suddenly turned to joy on May 7. In Reims, France, a representative of the German General Staff, which had taken control of the country after Hitler's death, accepted the terms of unconditional surrender. May 8 was proclaimed Victory in Europe Day.

President Truman, along with America's allies, now concentrated all of his efforts on winning the war against Japan in the Pacific. On August 6, the world's first atomic bomb was dropped on Hiroshima. Almost 180,000 people were killed. Three days later, a second atomic bomb was dropped on Nagasaki, with 80,000 casualties. On August 14, President Truman announced to the nation that the war was over. Japan officially surrendered on September 2.

Like most Americans, Freddie and his

family were looking forward to the postwar years as a time for things to get back to normal, but that wasn't to happen. Almost immediately, the United States was crippled by numerous labor strikes, including those by steel, coal mining, and railroad workers.

Although industrial and mining conflicts had been a part of the lives of all of the people of southwestern Pennsylvania for a long time, there was something about late 1945 and early 1946 that felt different to Freddie and his family. Everyone seemed to be talking more about the unions now. In fact, southwestern Pennsylvania was about to erupt in violence.

We Are All Neighbors

One evening at dinner, at the beginning of March 1946, Mr. Rogers and Grandfather McFeely expressed for the first time their concern about what would happen if the Brick and Clay Workers Local 437, from up in Armstrong County, succeeded in organizing the workers at the brick factory.

"I've talked to all the supervisors and foremen and told them how I feel about it," Mr. Rogers said. "They promised me they'd try to keep the union out."

"I hope they can keep that promise," Grandfather McFeely said.

Freddie laid down his fork. "Ding Dong, don't the workers at the brick factory have the right to join a union if they want to?" he asked.

"Well, it's kind of complicated, Freddie. They have the *right,* of course, but John L. Lewis usually goes too far and demands too many labor concessions that we don't think are good for business," Grandfather McFeely said. "Sometimes he makes it *them* against *us.*"

Freddie had a lot of friends whose fathers not only worked at the McFeely Brick Company, but in the coal mines and steel mills around Latrobe as well. With talks between labor and management breaking down almost daily, he wondered if they would soon think of him as one of the enemy.

Freddie decided that he was going to start running a series of editorials in the high school newspaper that would explain the history and importance of the labor movement.

When the editorials appeared, they provoked some angry comments from both teachers and students. Freddie and Mr. Hawkins had to spend some time in the principal's office, explaining why they thought the editorials were necessary. Everything that Freddie wrote was supported by facts and so well thought out that it was difficult for anyone to ignore his arguments.

Still, Freddie wasn't prepared for what happened on Tuesday, March 26. Workers at the Westinghouse Electric Corporation's east Pittsburgh plant went on strike, and when supervisors and foremen tried to enter the plant, a battle broke out between them and the strikers.

The sheriff and his deputies did their best to keep the situation under control, but tensions were so high that before long, they had to call in the state police to handle the strikers, whose strength had grown to 2,000. Two hundred and fifty troopers, mounted and on foot, were rushed from nearby Greensburg to break up the mob. Some Pittsburgh radio stations reported that several of the strikers were severely beaten, but that claim was disputed by the head of the Pennsylvania State Police.

The next day, when Freddie got to school, a crowd of students were milling around the entrance to the building.

He saw one of his reporters and hurried up to her. "What's going on, June?" he asked.

"We just had our own Westinghouse strike," June said. "Phil Green's dad is one of the supervisors at the plant, and Bob Fuller's dad is one of the workers. They got into a shoving match, which turned into a fight, which turned into a brawl, and now about ten students are in the principal's office."

Freddie shook his head in disbelief. "Can't people just talk these things out?" he said. "Can't people just lay out all of their differences on the table and then compromise for the good of all?"

"Apparently Phil and Bob can't, Freddie," June said. She looked around to see if anyone was listening to them. "And someone even mentioned your name right before you got here. A few people think your editorials may have started the Westinghouse strike."

Freddie gave her a disbelieving look. "Now, that is one of the craziest things I have ever heard in my life, that an editorial in a high school newspaper would cause workers at the Westinghouse plant in Pittsburgh to go on strike."

June shrugged. "I don't know if it is or not, Freddie," she said. "I'm sure that some students take copies of the newspaper home and maybe their parents read them. A lot of the teachers called your labor editorials 'thought provoking.' You really did make some very strong points on behalf of all working people."

Right then, the doors to the school opened. The crowd of students surged forward, but just as Freddie and June reached the door, Freddie felt a hand on his shoulder. When he looked up, he saw Mr. Hawkins. "We need to have a meeting," he whispered. "It's all right if you and June are late to math. I've already talked to Miss Wren."

Freddie and June followed Mr. Hawkins to his classroom.

When they got there, the rest of the staff were already seated at the tables where they worked on the newspaper.

Freddie and June sat down next to each other.

George Franklin looked over at Freddie and said, "Well, I hope you're satisfied, Rogers. Your editorials have gotten us all into a lot of trouble."

Freddie was just about to reply to George's remark, when Mr. Hawkins said, "How do you figure that, George?"

172

"Why else are we here?" George said. "You saw that crowd in front of the school, and you know what happened to Phil and Bob. It was the Westinghouse strike all over again." He looked around the room. "There were a lot of us here who didn't want those editorials to be published, but Rogers overruled us. Of course, I guess that'll stop now, because he must be in a lot of trouble."

For a few moments, no one said anything. Then Mr. Hawkins cleared his throat. "The administration of this high school does not believe that Freddie's editorials caused the problems this morning between Phil and Bob. In fact, the principal believes that Freddie's editorials on labor issues have given our students and faculty a better understanding of the problems this country will face in the postwar period. He told me that he wants the staff to write a series of editorials on how to get along with our neighbors, and, of course, as editor, Freddie will be the lead writer."

That night, at the dinner table, Freddie told his parents and Lainey what had happened at school and what the staff of the newspaper had been asked to do.

"Oh, Freddie, that is just wonderful!" Mrs. Rogers said.

"We're so proud of you, Freddie," Mr. Rogers added. "Do you have any idea what you're going to say?"

"Actually, I do, because I've been thinking about it ever since this morning," Freddie said. "I've not written anything down, but I do have most of the first editorial in my head. Would you like to hear it?"

"Will you tell us with a puppet?" Lainey asked.

"All right, if you want me to, Lainey, I can do that," Freddie said. He excused himself and went up to his room.

When he came back downstairs, he was holding a puppet he had made just the day before.

"That puppet looks just like you, Freddie," Lainey said.

Freddie grinned. He pulled the sock puppet over his hand, wiggled his fingers, which made Lainey giggle, and then said, in a puppet voice, "Every human being needs help at one time or another. Sometimes this help comes from a family member, but just as often it will come from a neighbor.

"As a neighbor, we all have something important to give to our other neighbors. We may not even realize that we're giving it, because our gift can be as simple as a smile or a wave of the hand.

"We don't have to like everyone in this world. But we can learn to be 'neighborly'—respectful, courteous, and kind to one another."

Freddie stopped. He pulled the puppet off his hand. "That's it," he said. "What do you think?"

For just a minute, no one said anything. Then Mr. Rogers stood up, walked over to where Freddie was standing, and put his arm around his shoulders. "I think that whoever your neighbors are in years to come are going to be very lucky people indeed."

Endings and Beginnings

Although the tensions caused by the Westinghouse Electric Company strike had not been totally forgotten, as the school year began to draw to a close, the members of the Latrobe High School Class of 1946 turned their attention to other things, such as passing all their classes and the senior prom.

One of Freddie's jobs, as president of the Student Council, was to make sure that the prom went off without a hitch. At a meeting of the prom committees one morning,

Freddie looked around the room and didn't see Jim Stumbaugh. Jim's committee was in charge of decorations.

When Freddie asked where Jim was, Jeanne Lowe said, "I thought everybody knew, Freddie. Jim had to go to the hospital last night for emergency surgery. It has something to do with an old football injury."

"Oh, I'm sorry to hear that," Freddie said. "Is he going to be all right?"

"We really won't know too much more until this afternoon," Jeanne answered, "but he'll probably have to stay in the hospital for two or three weeks."

Freddie hesitated for just a minute, then he said, "I hate to ask, especially at a time like this, Jeanne, but has the decoration committee decided on a theme?"

Jeanne nodded. "We had a meeting the day before Jim went to the hospital," she said. "We decided on 'South Seas.'"

Everyone nodded their agreement.

"That sounds great," Freddie said. "Well, if I can help in any way, just let me know."

The other committees gave their reports, and Freddie pronounced the plans for the prom were on schedule.

But as he headed home after school, Freddie couldn't get his mind off Jim Stumbaugh. Jim was Latrobe High School's Big Man on Campus. He was president of the senior class, captain of the football team, the top scorer on the basketball team, and one of the faster runners on the track team. He had it all. He was the idol of almost every male in school and the dream of almost every female. Jim's future was assured. He had been offered a football scholarship to Penn State, a basketball scholarship to the University of Michigan, and a track scholarship to Yale. Now, Jim was in the hospital, facing a very uncertain future.

When Freddie got to his house, he put his

books down on a table in the entry hall and went into the kitchen for a glass of water. His mother and Ruth were packing some food into a hamper.

"Is someone going on a picnic?" Freddie asked as he ran tap water in a glass. He grinned. "I'll be glad to carry the hamper."

"I'm sure you would, dear, but it would probably be empty before you got to the front door," Mrs. Rogers said. "No, these are just some things for a bake sale at Ruth's church tonight."

Freddie drank his water and then sat down at the table. "Mama, Jim Stumbaugh is in the hospital because he had an emergency operation last night."

"Oh, Freddie, I'm sorry to hear that," Mrs. Rogers said.

"Jeanne Lowe said he'll probably have to stay in the hospital for a few weeks," Freddie said. "I want to do something for him, but I can't think of anything."

"Why don't you take him his homework?" Mrs. Rogers suggested. "I think that would be very helpful."

Freddie thought for a minute. "To be honest, Mama, I don't know Jim well enough to do something like that," he said. "We just aren't in the same circles."

"Freddie, how will you ever know anyone really well if you don't make an effort to?" Mrs. Rogers said.

"Well, let me think about it," Freddie said.

"I'm sure you'll do the right thing, dear," Mrs. Rogers said. "You always do."

Freddie went upstairs to his room. He lay on his bed and wondered how Jim must be feeling right now. He tried to put himself in the same situation. Finally, he realized his mother was right.

At dinner, Freddie told Mr. Rogers about Jim's surgery. "When I finish eating, I'm going to the hospital to see him."

Mrs. Rogers smiled and nodded her head.

* * * *

When Freddie got to the Latrobe Area Hospital, he was told that Jim's room was on the third floor, so he took the elevator up.

Just as the doors opened, he met Jeanne and Betty Wilson, one of the cheerleaders who ran in the same circles as Jim. Both girls looked startled to see him.

"I'm here to visit Jim," Freddie explained.

"Well, that's really sweet of you, Freddie," Jeanne said. "I know he'll be glad to see you. But you probably shouldn't tire him out too much talking about the prom."

"Oh, I'm not here to talk about that," Freddie said. "I'm just here as a . . . well, friend."

When Freddie got to Jim's room, the radio was tuned to a baseball game. Jim's back was turned to the door, so he didn't see Freddie come in.

"Jim?" Freddie called softly.

"What? Who's that?" Jim said. "Come

around here on the other side, because it's hard for me to turn over."

Freddie walked around the bed. "Hi, Jim," he said.

Jim blinked a couple of times as though he couldn't believe he was seeing Freddie. "What are you doing here?"

"I came here to visit my friend," Freddie said.

"Oh?" Jim said. "What's he in for?"

"He had emergency surgery," Freddie replied.

"That makes two of us," Jim said. "How's your friend doing?"

"He looks like he's doing very well, but I'll ask him," Freddie said. "How are you doing, Jim?"

"What?" Jim said. After a few seconds, he added, "You mean you were talking about me?"

Freddie nodded. "How are you doing?" he repeated.

"Well, I'm still sore, but the doctors told

me that I'm going to be all right and that I should be able to play football again."

"Are you sure you want to?" Freddie said.

It took Jim a couple of minutes before he finally said, "No, I'm not. But you won't tell anybody, will you?"

"No, I won't tell anybody," Freddie said.

"Everybody still thinks I should accept that scholarship to Penn State," Jim said, "but . . . I can't believe I'm telling you all this, Freddie, since we hardly know each other, but I'm kind of tired of playing footfall, and I don't think I want to spend all of my time in college doing that."

"I understand," Freddie said. "I don't think there's anything that makes a person more unhappy than doing something he doesn't want to do, just because he thinks everybody else is expecting him to do it."

"Hey! That's exactly how I feel about it," Jim said. "You're the first person who's ever put it into words for me, though."

"Actually, another reason I came is I thought I'd ask if I could bring your homework to you," Freddie said. "It wouldn't be any problem, and that way, you could stay caught up. When you get back to school, it would almost be like you were never gone."

"You'd really do that for me?" Jim asked. "That's a lot of trouble."

"It wouldn't be any trouble at all, since we have several classes together," Freddie said. "I'd really like to do it for you."

"Thanks, Freddie. You're the only person who's even mentioned that," Jim said. "This is what real friendship is all about, I think."

After school the next Monday, Freddie went straight to the hospital. He had told Jim's teachers what he was doing, but he hadn't mentioned it to anyone else. When Freddie got to Jim's room, though, Jeanne and Betty were both there and gave him their biggest smiles.

"You are just the sweetest, most thoughtful person in the world, Freddie Rogers," Jeanne said.

Freddie could feel a deep blush coming on, but he managed to say, "Well, I'd like to think that if I had emergency surgery, somebody would do the same for me."

"I hope you never have this operation, Freddie," Jim said, "but if you do, I'll be there with your books and your assignments."

The next morning, everyone in school knew what Freddie had done. All of a sudden, he was a member of Jim's charmed circle of friends. Freddie enjoyed the new friendships because there were now more people than ever willing to help make sure the prom was the best one that Latrobe High School had ever had. But Freddie was mostly happy because he felt he had done something worthwhile for another human being.

❋   ❋   ❋

The rest of the school year seemed to race by, and for Freddie and everyone else in the senior class, June came too soon. Still, they all agreed that they had been looking forward to this day since they had first stepped through the doors of elementary school.

On graduation night, the senior class, dressed in their best clothes, marched into the auditorium to the strains of "Pomp and Circumstance" and took their seats in the front rows.

Several students had been asked to say a few words to the audience. Freddie was among them.

As he made his way to the steps leading up to the stage, he thought about how much he was going to miss his family and his high school friends. But he was looking forward to finding out what the future held for him at Dartmouth College.

When Freddie reached the podium, he laid down the paper on which he had written his speech, adjusted the microphone, and looked out into the audience.

"Often when we think we're at the end of something, we're really at the beginning of something else," Freddie said. "I've felt that way many times, and I'm feeling it now.

"My hope for the nineteen forty-six senior class of Latrobe High School, and indeed for everyone else in this auditorium, is that the 'miles we go before we sleep,' to quote Robert Frost, will be filled with all the feelings that come from deep caring—delight, sadness, joy, wisdom—and that in all the endings of our lives, we will always be able to see the new beginnings."

The Early Years in Television

Fred left Dartmouth College after one year and, much to the delight of his family, especially Grandfather McFeely, enrolled in Rollins College in Winter Park, Florida. In 1951, he graduated magna cum laude with a bachelor's degree in music composition.

That summer, he moved to New York City, where he got a job with the National Broadcasting Corporation working as an assistant producer and floor director for such television programs as *Your Lucky Strike Hit Parade, The Kate Smith Hour, The Voice of*

Firestone, and *The NBC Opera Theatre.*

On July 9, 1952, Fred married Sara Joanne Byrd, a fellow Rollins classmate.

In 1953, Fred and Joanne moved back to Pennsylvania, where Fred helped establish WQED, the public television station in Pittsburgh.

At first, Fred wasn't interested in children's television, but when nobody else wanted to produce it, he volunteered. He found a ready-made outlet for his puppetry when he and his friend Josie Carey produced the hour-long show called *The Children's Corner* for National Educational Television in 1954. It was this program that gave birth to a number of Fred's beloved puppet friends, including Daniel the Striped Tiger and King Friday XIII.

Fred and Joanne's two sons were born while they were living in Pittsburgh: James in 1959, and John in 1961.

During the seven years that Fred was the behind-the-scenes puppeteer, writer, and coproducer of *The Children's Corner,* he also worked part-time on his master of divinity degree at the Pittsburgh Theological Seminary. In 1962, he was ordained as a Presbyterian minister by the Pittsburgh Presbytery.

It was also during this time that Fred met Dr. Margaret McFarland. She had helped Dr. Benjamin Spock establish the child-care development program at the University of Pittsburgh in 1952. Dr. McFarland served as Fred's mentor when he enrolled in graduate work in the child-care development program. After he finished his studies, he stayed in contact with Dr. McFarland, and she became an informal consultant on his television show.

In 1963, Fred and his family moved to Toronto, Ontario, Canada, when the Canadian Broadcasting Corporation (CBC) offered him the opportunity to create a fifteen-minute children's program called *Mister Rogers.* Fred not only developed and produced the show, but he hosted it as well, marking his first time appearing in front of the television camera. Many of the elements that he incorporated into this program he would later use in *Mister Rogers' Neighborhood.*

In 1965, Fred moved his family back to Pennsylvania. Since he had obtained the broadcast rights to all the *Mister Rogers* episodes from the CBC, he decided to combine them into half-hour segments called *Mister Rogers' Neighborhood.* This new show was broadcast on WQED in Pittsburgh from 1965 until 1967. In 1967, the Sears-Roebuck Foundation agreed to fund the program, and it became available to every public television station in the United States.

Mister Rogers

When *Mister Rogers' Neighborhood* was first televised nationally in early 1968, viewers realized it was unlike any other children's show on television. Fred Rogers actually talked *to* preschoolers, not *at* them. He was genuinely interested in their lives and their problems, and the children responded to that. Each show was about a child's individual needs and feelings. Just as his grandfather McFeely had done for him years before, Fred tried to make the young people who watched the program understand that they were very important and that he liked them just the way they were. He did this by constantly reinforcing their self-worth and reminding them that they were special and that they were loved.

Fred purposely made the pace of *Mister Rogers' Neighborhood* leisurely. Things happened in real time. He had no use for the flashy and fast-paced programming of some other children's television shows. In *Mister Rogers' Neighborhood*, a comforting routine starts off each episode. Fred enters the set and begins to sing the show's theme song, which asks the viewers to be his neighbor. As he sings, Fred changes from his sports coat and dress shoes to a cardigan sweater and sneakers. One of the sweaters that his mother knitted for him now hangs in a permanent collection of the Smithsonian Institution in Washington, D.C.

During each episode of *Mister Rogers' Neighborhood*, different guests and neighbors drop by to talk about how to deal with the different feelings and emotions that we all have. The daily journey by trolley to the "Neighborhood of Make-Believe" is also an important part of each show. Here, puppets like Daniel Striped Tiger, King Friday XIII, Queen Sara, and Lady Elaine help viewers deal with different feelings and emotions in a fantasy setting.

Over the years, in addition to the *Mister Rogers' Neighborhood* televison program, Fred was involved in other projects. He made six children's music albums. He also wrote several books for and about preschoolers. These books deal with real-life events, such as going to school, going to the doctor, going to day care, stepfamilies, and the death of loved ones. Such issues form the basis for the more than seven hundred episodes of *Mister Rogers' Neighborhood.*

In recognition of his tireless effort to improve the quality of children's programs on television, Fred was honored with numerous

196

awards, including two Peabodys and three Emmys. He also received thirty honorary doctorates from universities and colleges throughout the United States. Experts in the field of child study have praised Fred's natural ability to relate to preschoolers.

At the beginning of the Gulf War in 1991, Fred taped spots for Public Broadcasting Service to help young people understand that they would be safe during the hostilities. In 1997, Fred was honored for lifetime achievement by the National Academy of Television Arts and Sciences and by the Television Critics Association. The following year, Fred was honored with a star on the Hollywood Walk of Fame. In 1999, Fred was inducted into the Television Hall of Fame.

Fred announced his retirement in the fall of 2000. After a run of thirty-four years, the final episode of *Mister Rogers' Neighborhood* aired on Friday, August 31, 2001.

In 2002, Fred was presented with the

Presidential Medal of Freedom, the nation's highest civilian honor. That same year, he filmed several public service announcements for PBS to help young people deal with the first anniversary of the September 11, 2001, terrorist attacks.

Fred continued to write children's books and to work on his Web site, which featured parenting advice, until his death from cancer on February 27, 2003.

In November 2003, Fred was posthumously inducted into the Broadcasting and Cable Hall of Fame.

Fortunately for future generations of preschoolers, *Mister Rogers' Neighborhood* will continue in reruns for many years to come. PBS plans to draw from a rotating library of more than three hundred episodes.

Fred McFeely Rogers will still be coming into everyone's living room, putting on his cardigan sweater and sneakers, and asking, "Will you be my neighbor?"

FOR MORE INFORMATION

Collins, Mark, and Margaret Mary Kimmel, editors. *Mister Rogers' Neighborhood: Children, Television, and Fred Rogers.* Pittsburgh: University of Pittsburgh Press, 1996.

DiFranco, JoAnn, and Anthony DiFranco. *Mister Rogers: Good Neighbor to America's Children.* Minneapolis: Dillon Press, 1983.

Rogers, Fred, and Barry Head. *Mister Rogers Talks with Parents.* Pittsburgh: Family Communications, Inc., 1983.

Rogers, Fred. *You Are Special.* Philadelphia: Running Press, 2002.

Rogers, Fred. *The World According to Mister Rogers: Important Things to Remember.* New York: Hyperion, 2003.

There are also a lot of Web sites that you can access by typing in the words "Fred Rogers" on any search engine.